Sweet Lori

Clifton LaBree

© 2007 by Author, Clifton LaBree

Published by
Fading Shadows Imprint
New Boston, New Hampshire

ISBN-10: 1943329133
ISBN-13: 978-1-943329-13-7

Cover Design by Vivian LaBree

Dedicated to my wife Pauline, and my family, with thanks for all their support and encouragement.

Chapter One

Kenneth Morgan asked the cab driver to drop him off at the road that had once led to the airfield with the small square control tower. He brushed away the small weeds and saplings that had grown in the roadway until he saw the field and the squat tower with the observation platform on the roof. He paused and stared at the scene. It was as he remembered it. Visions of his service at the field were stored in a very private place in his consciousness, shared with very few. Now that those deeply held memories struggled to be acknowledged, he was overcome by their intensity.

His heart pounded, and instantly he was emotionally transported to twenty years before when the world was on fire and nations were intent on destroying each other. Memories he had long suppressed opened up to him in torrents. Once again, he was a young pilot flying B-17 Flying Fortresses on daylight bombing missions to destroy Germany's war-making machine. In the midst of all the terror and anxiety that the war was capable of, there was also a camaraderie that had held his crew of ten men into a tightly-knit band of brothers who supported and encouraged each other. At times, they were capable of joking and laughing simply to hide their fears and horrors of the unknown. When tragedy struck, those who were alive held the rest of the crew together, emotionally and physically.

It was impossible to stand alone; the terror was too strong, so they all drew strength from the group, even though they covered the spectrum of social, educational and financial backgrounds. Their common bond made their Flying Fortress one of the best instruments of destruction in the squadron. It created a time and place that all of the veterans were unable to duplicate in their daily lives after the war. That bond of brotherhood transcended every measure of human involvement, and many yearned, at some time, to experience that same level of belonging to a part of history that was fast eroding memories of how it had been. The disappointment of never finding that same level of commitment to a cause greater than self inevitably left a yearning to recapture that same spirit of sharing, protecting, and belonging. It was a unique human trait treasured by all who experienced it.

The energy and excitement that had permeated the airfield was still there. Ken could feel it in his bones. It made him tingle all over. If he closed his eyes he could still feel the vibrations of heavy bombers warming up for a mission on the runway while others were propelled down the field with engines roaring at full throttle, laboring to lift the heavily laden craft into the air. Everyone held their breath praying that the engines would not stumble or misfire during the initial climb after takeoff. Powerful Wright Cyclone radial engines built by the Studebaker Motor Company settled into a steady pitch as the ground dropped away from the plane. An immediate feeling of freedom had always accompanied that moment for Ken. The thrill of flight was an integral part of his being.

They leveled off to a cruising speed at about ten thousand feet, and the squadron formed up into their box formations. Their time over the English Channel could be a boring part of the round trip, but most of the men filled their minds with thoughts of home and hearth, and especially of loved ones. A normal bombing run constituted hours of uncertainty and boredom that instantly changed into unadulterated terror. Fear and anxiety of the unknown were constant companions, and few tried to hide their emotions. Some talked too much about insignificant things while others, like Ken, kept his council. He readily announced his concern and fear to the men, yet he recognized that he had to set an example of positive thinking in the face of unspeakable horrors. That was his hardest role.

Once they left the relative security of the Channel and were in the air space over fortress Europe, every man began his private time in purgatory. Sitting at ten thousand feet above enemy territory in a small capsule of complex American machinery that constituted the plane, each man was in a private world of pure unmitigated personal terror. No one was immune to the reality. It was up to every man to handle the emotions that were as normal on every mission as eating and breathing.

* * *

Ken slowly walked across the runway with broken pieces of concrete invaded by grasses and shrubbery of every description. He could recall how the ground vibrated when the squadron was taking off or landing. The control tower was the center of their world during the war. At the far end of the field, he could see that corn was growing where the second of three runways had once been. Off to the side had been a graveyard area filled with broken planes and spare parts. Now it had small saplings over six inches in diameter.

The tower, however, was much as he remembered it. The iron railings around the observation platform were a little more rusty now, but they were still sturdy and whole. Climbing the stairs, Ken thought he could hear that peculiar drone of large aircraft approaching the field like a huge wave of sound getting closer and closer. He looked into the eastern sky to see if he was dreaming, but it was only a figment of his imagination. Many times over the years he had experienced similar echoes from the past. Sometimes the planes were so badly damaged, the crews did not bother to follow the normal landing pattern and came straight in for what was frequently a crash landing. At every airfield in England there were three runways arranged in a triangle, so that aircraft in trouble could pick the one most suitable for their plane.

He remembered that sick feeling that every person on the ground had when they saw the crippled planes struggling to stay airborne. Those that were whole came in and made a complete turn to land on the runway in front of the tower. The other two were reserved for cripples. It was amazing what German fighters and ground anti-aircraft fire could do to the planes. Many were flying coffins with death and mangled young bodies on board. Occasionally a plane would make it to the ground and suddenly explode in a firestorm of flame. The fiery holocausts were a sight that never left him. Grim-faced ground crews waited anxiously for their planes to return, hoping that the black spot on the horizon might be it, bringing their buddies and friends back from one more mission.

The sweet smell of burning bodies inside the fiery pyres was a lasting legacy. Once you experienced it, you never forgot it. Ken bent over the railing to support himself and retched, but nothing came up. Images and sounds were passing through his body like a fast running mountain stream flowing over a waterfall, obeying the basic law of gravity.

Ken sat down on a bench near the railing and began to fill his pipe, reminiscing about the most notable period of his life when he was a young captain, pilot and commander of the Flying Fortress he and the crew had affectionately named "Sweet Lori" after his newly born daughter in Maine.

There had been three separate planes to bear that proud name. The faces of his first crew were still fresh in his memory, well aware that every pilot reflected favorably on their first crew. There had been several crews over the three years, but his first had left a more enduring legacy, especially the belly turret gunner called Lewis Whalen. Lew was a short, small-framed eighteen-year-old young man with a nose covered with freckles and a mop of bright red hair. He was the epitome of the laid-back Maine Yankee. It took a lot to get him excited. He was the most calm and collected young man Ken had ever known.

Lew was away from home for the first time and was extremely homesick. Ken noted that he was having a difficult time and struck up a relationship on the fact that they were the only two men from Maine in the squadron. That bonded their friendship and made it unique. Lew quickly fitted into the routines of the squadron and became a valuable member. He had graduated from gunnery school with high praise. In combat, he was tenacious in fighting back at the swarms of German fighters intent in destroying the bomber. Lew seemed to take it personal. Ken learned that his father had been wounded in the First World War and had a long-standing hatred towards anything German.

Soon after Lew's arrival with the crew, he was promoted to a corporal and took great delight in sewing on his stripes. He was defensive and sensitive about his stature, but he was not pugnacious. He was worried about being afraid and had confided to Ken one day that the other crewmen would think him a coward. Ken was quick to inform him that everybody was frightened and that fear was a natural emotion that was beneficial in heightening awareness in times of danger, making a person more alert and more willing, even anxious, to fight back. The adrenalin that pumped through their veins during combat pushed fear temporarily to one side so that more rational thinking could take place. It was a response veterans made every time they entered combat.

Ken had flown thirty-six bombing missions as a pilot from the airfield located in Anglia. He could remember almost every mission for its uniqueness rather than it being the target or the fight to and from the target. The original "Sweet Lori" made half of the trips until it became another casualty and was added to the growing pile of scrap metal.

That last flight of the original "Sweet Lori" was seared into his memory like a laser, and was just as real today as when it was taking place. It had shattered his sanity for a while. Just recalling the details made him grow cold all over. They had just dropped their payload on the strategic targets and were headed for home, still over eastern Germany when they were hit, wham, wham wham. The two waist gunners, the top turret gunner, the radio operator and the navigator were all wounded by the AA fire. Two died from loss of blood shortly after the ground fire had severely ripped the bottom of the fuselage open. Ken immediately dropped to a lower altitude, or the wounded would freeze from the cold drafts entering the shattered plane.

Most of the electrical equipment was inoperable and the hydraulic system that raised and lowered the landing gear was ruptured. Ken ordered the crew to manually crank down the gear. They reported that it was stuck with only one wheel in lockdown position. That message sent spikes of terror through him. One wheel... He had only two engines left. It was a struggle to keep the aircraft afloat, and he ordered the crew to ditch everything that could be dismantled including the ammunition and machine guns.

Then he sent a message to Lew, "Corporal, I want you to get out of your turret and help the crew lighten the ship, and put your parachute on."

Lew tried to turn his turret facing toward the rear so that he could open the hatch in the floor of the plane, but nothing happened. He tried again and called in a hysterical voice, "Captain, I can't make it. The swing mechanism is jammed, and I can't move it manually."

The message rang in Ken's ears, making him nauseous. Just then he noted the presence of two P-51 Mustang fighter planes straddling him, and momentarily he felt some relief. "Bomber to escort," he called over his radio. "Do you read me?"

"We read you 'Sweet Lori' and will accompany you all the way back to base."

"Would you look me over and give me an assessment of the damage? Our hydraulic and electrical systems are out, and the belly turret is jammed in place," Ken requested, trying to be as calm as possible over the radio.

"Captain, I can't get out of here," Lew cried again in a high pitched voice.

"Sweet Lori, this is Mustang One. You've been badly damaged, as you must already know. You have only one

6

wheel down, and you're leaking gas from the main gas tank. Good luck."

"Roger, escort," Ken had replied. "Lew, keep trying to free the mechanism. Pilot to rest of crew. See if there is any way you can cut a hole into the belly turret so that the safety hatch can be opened."

With that order given, Ken had his hands full flying the plane and keeping the engines operating at peak efficiency or they were not going to make it to base. Even if they were lucky enough to get to base, he would end up crushing Lew with only one wheel down. "Why me?" he cried.

The thought of what he would do to the young man from Maine made him sick all over. He prayed to and cursed at the God that left him with no options to save Lew. Even if he ditched the plane in the Channel, Lew would drown...

All the way across the Atlantic Lew begged for one of the crew to shoot him rather than have him ground up like hamburger. He didn't want to take a chance that he might survive the mangling and become a mass of disfigured flesh.

Ken tried to think of something he could say to Lew, but words failed him. Screams and cries for help pierced the fuselage of the aircraft as it slowly came in view of the white cliffs of Dover. Watching the terrain below, Ken came up with the idea of landing the plane while straddling one of the irrigation ditches in the agricultural fields around the base. He remembered that there was one close by the main runway he could approach without difficulty. He announced the decision to the crew. They had to make it on the first pass because he did not have enough power or fuel to go around for a second attempt.

The two banks on the drainage ditch were higher than the surrounding corn fields. That brought some relief to Ken who planned on placing the body of the aircraft in the center of the ditch, which had enough depth to allow the belly turret to pass in safety, provided the wings were strong enough to hold the plane onto the banks. It was a gamble, but it was the only option available.

Without another thought, Ken called for the crew to secure themselves for a belly landing. "Lew, can you hear me?"

"Yes," he replied in a wavering voice. "I understand what you're trying to do, Sir. In case it doesn't work, promise me that you'll personally inform my mother and father? If I had my sidearm I'd finish the job myself rather than take a chance of being crushed like a grape..." A long cry of despair shattered the relative quiet of the lumbering Flying Fortress.

It completely unnerved everyone who was listening in on the conversation. Ken sat at the controls of the wounded aircraft praying from the bottom of his soul for some miracle from his God to give him a chance to bring the plane in without killing or maiming their young friend and comrade who still had so much to live for.

Ken had always accepted his responsibility for the safety of the crew as a sacred trust. He called the escort Mustangs to relay his landing plan to the control tower. The engines were breaking down. He was having trouble keeping the plane in a straight line, wondering if the plane was capable of staying airborne until he reached the cornfield. Aware of the potential for disaster, Ken tried to block everything out of his mind and concentrate on getting down safely. Ripping his headgear off he lifted up on the left wing so that he could better see the ground.

In the distance he recognized two church steeples lined up in a row and knew that he was on the correct flight path. The plane was vibrating so badly everyone was afraid it was about to disintegrate. Breathing was now difficult and his tongue was swollen from dryness and worry. The throttles were at maximum speed, yet they were still losing altitude. The co-pilot frantically played with manifold pressure and carburetor mixture to determine the most efficient setting, to no avail.

Two minutes after landfall, he saw the airfield and the ditch to the west of the main runway. He slightly nudged the throttle back to a speed sufficient to keep them airborne, making his approach low and as slow as possible; then he killed the engines. A powerless landing would have less effect on the structural integrity of the aircraft. A few feet from the ground he lowered the full flaps to slow them down as much as possible before impact. His aim was perfect. The fuselage was directly over the center of the ditch. With his tail flaps down full, the plane's tail wheel was the first to touch the ground in the ditch and had the potential to act as a steering rudder to keep the plane centered.

The wings made contact with the ground shortly after the tail wheel, kicking up dust that choked everyone on board. So far, so good. Ken thought they had a chance of making it when the right wing caught on a rock, causing the craft to pivot in a semi-circle around the lodged wing. The maneuver pulled the belly turret into the opposite bank, sheering it from the fuselage so that it rolled beneath the heavy bomber with Lew inside. Ken heard nothing, but later, the rest of the crew admitted to hearing one loud cry from Lew and then silence.

Once the plane came to a stop, Ken was unable to move from his seat. Within seconds ground crew members were spraying foam over the craft to prevent fire. The medics had to cut Ken's harness free of his seat and carried him to a waiting ambulance. He remained in a comatose state for twenty-four hours, unable to move or speak.

The five men that survived the crash came to visit him in the Quonset hut infirmary, trying hard to put on a positive demeanor. He saw them, but when he opened his mouth to speak, nothing came out. Tears welled in his eyes and rolled down into his ears; an intense feeling of shame and self-loathing consumed him. The men wearily trudged out of the hut and were intercepted by the flight surgeon who questioned them about Captain Morgan's condition and what took place on the flight. They explained to him about Corporal Lew Whalen and left, each of them horrified about his loss and the way it took place. None ever placed blame on the captain, for he did all that was humanely possible to save poor Lew.

9

The next day, Ken awoke to the familiar sound of Wright Cyclone engines filling the air, another flight warming up for the day's mission. The pace was relentless and never ending until the Germans capitulated. Replacement crews filed into the squadron in large numbers. There were no old veterans, just those who had been lucky, which included Ken. Statistically he should have been a casualty of the air war against the Germans; it was simply a question of time. The bomber groups had suffered the highest casualty rate of any other members of the United States armed forces in the war.

Ken threw the sheets off him and walked to the single window of the Quonset hut to watch the planes take off. One at a time the slow, lumbering Fortresses gathered speed down the runway and lifted off - destination Germany. One at a time they flew into the rising sun to the east and disappeared. He was with them emotionally as they crossed the Channel and into "flack alley" soon after entering France.

* * *

Now, twenty years later, Ken could still recall the pain and agony he experienced that morning. In his delirium he had asked his God to take him home so that he would not have to wake up to the reality of his responsibility.

The kindly doctor silently joined him at the window. They watched until all of the planes had taken off. He remembered that there were three aborts and twelve planes missing; one of them was "Sweet Lori".

"How are you feeling this morning?" the doctor asked in a calm, clear voice, recognizing the symptoms of a man on the edge of madness.

"How am I supposed to feel?" he had replied angrily.

"I can't answer that, Captain. I understand your anger and your trauma. Under the circumstances it's perfectly normal, even healthy. We all need a safety valve to relieve pain so monstrous that it would destroy us if not vented. We want to help you. I'm sending you home for a while to rest; you've certainly earned it after eighteen missions. I just spoke to your squadron commander, and he approves of my decision."

The magic word "home" had momentarily displaced his rage and irritation, and he began to shake all over until darkness enveloped him. He would have fallen to the floor if the doctor had not caught him. A nurse had been standing nearby. She assisted the doctor in placing his small, thin frame on the cot and covered him with a sheet.

Several days later, after long stretches of drug-induced sleep, Ken awoke, anxious to get out of the infirmary. His furlough was approved anytime he was strong enough to take it. The squadron commander had promised him a new plane when he returned. Qualified pilots were becoming scarce. Ken warmed to the proposal and asked for Lew Whalen's service file so that he could review the contents. He had promised Lew to visit his family, and Ken now saw that as his primary responsibility to the young gunner's memory. Lew and Ken had talked a lot about Maine.

Lew came from a small town called Sanford, not too far away from Gray where he and his wife Lorraine had built a log cabin on a lake. Thinking about the visit to Lew's family made him apprehensive. Here he was, a man barely holding on to his own sanity, and he was expected to bring some consolation and solace to a devastated family. He was a pathetic figure to fulfill such a role, especially when he had been the instrument of death!

Chapter Two

Ken's first stop after landing in the United States was a visit to the Whalen family. Walking up to the door of Lew's family home, Ken had felt terribly inadequate about the task ahead of him. It was a small New England style home in a rural setting. He had recovered somewhat from the trauma of the crash and looked from all outward appearances fit and trim in his newly tailored uniform with several rows of ribbons on his chest beneath his prized silver wings. He was praying for this visit to go well. Aside from all of the agony, there was something therapeutic with the visit. It was fulfilling a promise to a beloved crew member, and he always took promises seriously.

It was a warm, sunny day in June with the aroma of a freshly mowed lawn filling the air. He had called ahead to the family to prepare them for his arrival and made an appointment for 1:00 PM so that he would not interfere with their lunch. He knocked on the door on the front porch. A tall, slender man with intense dark eyes and a receding hairline answered the door.

"Hello, I'm Captain Morgan…"

"Welcome, Captain. I'm Lew's father, Lester Whalen," holding out his hand to Ken. "My wife, Natalie, and I have been expecting you. She's in the living room."

Ken shook his hand, removed his cap and followed Lester Whalen into the living room. He could smell fresh coffee being brewed as he walked a narrow hallway leading to the kitchen. It was a solemn moment for the three of them. Idle chatter would have been inappropriate. Mrs. Whalen was sitting on the couch, a petite lady with graying hair and dark luminous eyes. He thought how Lew had favored his mother in size and looks.

She rose from the couch to greet him. "Welcome to our home, Captain Morgan. Our son wrote often about you in his letters. He was pleased to have been assigned to your plane." The words were difficult for her. She looked up at him with pressed lips. A film of tears blinded her vision.

Lester Whalen took her into his arms to comfort her. Stroking her short hair, he tenderly suggested, "Maybe the Captain would like a cup of coffee, Natalie."

"That would be fine," Ken added, self-conscious of having witnessed their very private grief. "Soldiers never seem to get enough of it."

Mrs. Whalen released her husband and motioned toward the kitchen. "Why don't we go into the kitchen then. I baked some apple turnovers right after you called earlier, Captain. They were Lew's favorite. We can sit around the kitchen table if you don't mind."

"The kitchen at my home was the most used room in the house. I prefer it, Mrs. Whalen. I grew up in northern Maine, and some of my fondest childhood memories centered around a kitchen table very much like your lovely oak tavern table."

"Lew had told us about you and he being the only men from Maine in your squadron," Lester Whalen motioned for him to take a seat at the table. He had taken one beside his wife opposite Ken. Mrs. Whalen set out cups and plates for the turnovers and coffee and took her place at the table.

"The turnovers and coffee smell inviting, Mrs. Whalen. Thank you."

Lester Whalen fidgeted with his coffee cup and looked directly into Ken's eyes and asked, "The army would not tell us how Lew died, except that it was in a bombing raid. It's now been almost two months since his death. I believe we can accept the reality better if we knew what happened. When he joined the army right out of high school, we tried to mentally prepare ourselves for the worst case possible, but I can tell you that we had no idea how devastating it would be. The empty longing seems to get worse as time goes by, and life has lost its meaning for us. Lew was our life… Anything you can tell us about his last mission will be appreciated. Knowledge can be comforting when contrasted to the unknown."

Ken knew that the visit would evolve around how Lew died. How could he tell them? Just telling them the truth would paint an image of the desecration of his body that would probably never leave them. He looked at the two parents with the sad beseeching eyes and silently prayed for God to guide him with the right words at this hour of need.

"The army told us that you were hospitalized after the last mission, and that as soon as you were capable of making the trip, you had requested permission to visit us," Mrs. Whalen told him. "We've been counting the days since that moment, and now you're here…"

"What you say is true, Mrs. Whalen," Ken began. He was searching for the right words, but found no substitute for telling the truth head on. "Our last mission over Germany was successful, but our plane, a B-17, took a lot of AA fire and was severely damaged by German fighter planes going to and returning from German-controlled territory. Several of our crew were killed outright…"

"Was Lew one of those casualties?" Lester Whalen asked.

"No," Ken continued, choosing his words carefully. "Lew survived the trip to and from the target, but his belly turret was damaged, and we could not extract him from the enclosure. We were fortunate to bring the plane back to England where I made the decision to crash land in a farmer's field with a drainage ditch which had the potential of allowing Lew to survive the landing. It almost worked, until the right wing caught on a rock or some snag and whipsawed the plane into the bank of the drainage ditch, crushing your son who was still inside."

Even today, twenty years later, Ken could still see the anguish and horror on the faces of Lew's mother and father. The brutal violation of their son's body solicited a cry of pain from both of them. His mother wailed and cried, getting up to leave the room. Mr. Whalen was dumbfounded and followed after his wife, leaving Ken alone in the kitchen, numbed by the ordeal.

He had told the truth; they deserved that, even if he had left out some of the more ghastly aspects of the crash. He heard them both release the grief that had been building. Lester Whalen, the more composed of the two, consoled his wife, and twenty minutes later they returned to the table.

"Tell me, Captain, I'm no fool as to what happened. Tell me… was his death painless and quick?"

"Lew's death came instantly. Believe me, he had no time to feel any pain, and that is the truth," Ken replied, grasping the bereaved father in his arms. "I knew that I was going to be the messenger of pain, and I understand your grief. He was one of my crew, and I lost him for all of us. He has joined a select group of heroes that will remain forever young. I loved your son like a brother and share your sorrow." Tears came slowly at first, then in torrents. It was an intense moment of release that cleaned his soul, and for the first time since the crash, Ken was able to think rationally about the future.

Ken had spent several hours with the Whalen family just listening to them talk about events in Lew's life. They had a desperate desire to talk about him, and he found it reassuring to listen to their memories of a beloved son who the rescue crews found in pieces scattered along the drainage ditch. Ken never elaborated about the crash, but he had a feeling that they understood and neither pressed him for added descriptions.

He left the Whalen's home in Sanford and slowly walked to the army sedan completely drained emotionally and physically. Ken was surprised at his lack of stamina and had an urgent desire to be by himself for a while. He had picked up the army sedan at the Grenier Field motor pool in Manchester, New Hampshire, with permission to use the vehicle for the next four days, when he had to report for transport to England.

Returning to Maine had been a bittersweet event for him. After the ordeal at the Whalen's home, he was looking forward to a short respite with his wife, Lorraine, and daughter, Lori, whom he had never seen. Turning the Ford sedan north on US Route 1, Ken had headed toward Gray, north of Portland. Slowly the familiar surroundings began to register with him. The anticipation of seeing his family finally overshadowed all the ugliness that had overburdened him.

It was midday and he dismissed the urge to phone ahead, wanting to surprise Lorraine. Her warm and caring ways were all he had to cling to. Their love for each other had been the salvation of his soul. They had been high school sweethearts and had married after two years of college at the University of Maine. That had been in 1939. Even then there were tensions building in the world, so he had joined the Reserve Officer Training Corps which helped defray some of his tuition costs. They knew that when he graduated in 1941, he would have to fulfill his obligation of active service in the regular army. He was commissioned a second lieutenant early that summer when Lorraine informed him that she was pregnant. It was a joyful time for each of them. They planned for the future by purchasing a small hunting log cabin situated on a lake near their hometown. He and his father spent a lot of time that last spring he was in school, getting the cabin winterized so that they could live comfortably year round. They built a separate shed and garage attached to the original structure and partitioned off two rooms out of the great room of the cabin. It was small but comfortable, and, most of all, affordable on their limited budget, and they both loved its cozy interior.

Their daughter Lori was born two weeks after Pearl Harbor when he was attending flight school in Maryland. Normally he would have had a short furlough after earning his silver wings at graduation, but the war changed everything. He was immediately sent to England to join the bomber command being established there. He had moved into a recently built corrugated steel Quonset hut in the Anglia region of the country north of London at a town called Dunham. Thirty other junior officers were in the same hut.

Lorraine wrote every day without exception, keeping him up-to-date on little Lori's progress and miscellaneous gossip from their small town. The letters were a bright spot in a day filled with chaotic activity as he became capable of handling a B-17 four-engine bomber. Pictures Lorraine sent of Lori were precious to him, and he proudly shared them with his friends and buddies. She had the same sparkling dark eyes capable of expressing every emotion known to humans, just like her mother, and the same sandy brown hair which Lorraine usually did up in braids.

Lorraine's hair was always cut short just below the ears. She was an attractive girl with an allusive air of detachment which was her way of defending her privacy. There was depth to her that even Ken had never been able to define. Her serious nature gave her a sort of standoffish air, which discouraged familiarity; yet, her many friends admired her strength of character. While Ken studied forestry at Orono, she took education and became certified the year they married, taking a teaching job in Bangor while he continued his studies at Orono. It really helped with the family finances.

Their love for each other had developed over a long period of time. He came to love her for the aura of serenity that seemed to engulf them when they were together. Ken always admitted that she was the stronger personality of the two, and he depended on her strength more than he realized. Life was good back in those simple days when strong values and principles guided most people's lives. They made a perfect couple, and he was so anxious to recapture again, for a few days, that tranquility which emanated from her when he was with her. How dearly he loved the mother of his daughter!

It was late in the afternoon when Ken had turned off the main road into the driveway leading through a tall stand of majestic white pine trees to their cabin. He noticed an automobile parked near the cabin in a small pullout from the main driveway. He did not recognize the Hudson Terraplane automobile, and thought nothing about it.

The familiar sights brought back all the joy he remembered of belonging somewhere, and here he was experiencing it once again. It was a moment in which he thanked his God for sparing him when so many, like Lew

Whalen, were taken. Gone were the sick feelings of guilt and blame that had been the center of his existence since the crash. Here he could find peace and contentment away from the rest of the world. It was a retreat to nourish his soul and now, more than ever, he was in need of the healing powers and the saving grace. Just the thought of holding his wife and daughter in his arms sent shivers down his spine.

Their 1941 Studebaker Champion coupe was parked in the garage he had built. Everything was as he had remembered it. The soft murmur of the wind sifting through the tall white pine trees was soothing music to his ears. He had finally come home all in one piece after surviving eighteen difficult bombing missions over enemy territory. It was an exquisite moment. He removed his hat, flinging it on the Ford's seat and ran for the steps leading to the porch and the door leading to the kitchen.

Tears of joy filled Ken's eyes as he opened the screen door to the kitchen and let himself in. It was empty, so he continued into the great room of the cabin with the large fieldstone fireplace he had repaired before they had moved in. He paused to look around and to feel the warmth and security he always felt in the room. Nothing had changed except for the presence of a high chair and a few small stuffed toys on the couch near the fireplace. Off to the left was the room he had built for the baby. He quietly tiptoed to open the door to look inside, anticipating the first view of his daughter Lori. The room was empty. He partially closed the door behind him and walked to their bedroom where he heard muffled sounds and quietly opened the door.

After all the years that had passed, Ken could not recall exactly what he did. The image of his wife in bed with a stranger was forever seared in his consciousness. Lorraine and the stranger saw him the second he crossed the doorsill. At that moment he had the strongest urge to vomit and was afraid he would make a fool of himself. All he could do was stare at the unbelievable scene before him. His wife... his Lorraine... with another man in his bed... in his home!

18

A rage stronger than his ability to control it began to build within Ken. His first impulse was to approach the bed and grab the stranger by the hair of his head and fling him onto the floor near the door, prepared to kill him with his bare hands, but the man was quick on his feet and bolted from the cabin before Ken had a chance to think of his next move. He was afraid to look at Lorraine... stunned beyond comprehension. Oh how he hated her for this betrayal... "Where's my daughter?"

"Lori is with your mother and father for the day... I... I...didn't know you were coming home, Ken..."

"Obviously," he sneered in a loud voice.

"Ken... Ken... Please listen to me... listen to me... " She saw the horror in her husband's eyes and buried her head in her arms and wept. She kept saying over and over again, "My God no... no... Ken..."

He couldn't stand to hear her apologize and turned to leave. At the door he confronted her, "I better leave or I'll regret what I do. Don't try to explain anything to me. I want you to know how much I hate you for this. I'm warning you to clear out... You're not going to do this to me again, not in this house anyway..." Words failed him, and he ran from the cabin to the Ford sedan.

In a complete state of shock and rage, he started the car and left the driveway, anxious to leave the scene of the offensive betrayal of trust. There had to be some form of retribution and justice. In his anger Ken had forgotten all about little Lori and simply drove and drove until he was blinded by tears. He pulled off the road and purged himself of the poison he had witnessed. It was dark before Ken had dried his eyes and blown his nose with a clean handkerchief. In his tortured mind he had come up with a plan of action commensurate with the situation he had witnessed. It was something short of a physical attack that, at that moment, seemed to fit.

He turned the Ford around in the middle of the road and drove rapidly back to the cabin, half hoping to find Lorraine there. Either way, he was intent on burning the cabin to the ground. Her unfaithful act desecrated whatever they had shared, and he could no longer call such a place his home. Turning in the driveway, the first thing he noticed was that the Studebaker was gone. In a way, he thought, it made the job easier. Running onto the porch he didn't try to see if the door was locked; he smashed it open with his shoulder and ran into the great room.

He grabbed the two kerosene hurricane lamps off the fireplace mantel, smashing them on the floor in front of the couch. Then he grabbed some newspaper and crumpled it up in his hand, setting it on fire with his Zippo lighter and threw it on the floor where it burst into flames. He threw the couch pillows and some of the bedding from their bed in a pile on the snapping flames to make sure it was going to burn hot enough to consume the cabin. He watched the flames build and left the room, anxious to get as far away as possible.

Chapter Three

Ken headed north toward his parents' home in a daze, haunted by the revelations that stung him deeper and with more pain than anything he had ever experienced. The Lew Whalen disaster paled in comparison. He thought that if he brought his problem to his mother and father and they saw him in this confused condition, it would only worry them. Therefore, he detoured to a spot which he had visited frequently in his youth, sometimes with Lorraine.

It was a prominent overlook of a portion of the same lake as the cabin with a westerly view of the distant White Mountains in New Hampshire. He had come often to simply sit and think things out and always left in a more positive frame of mind than when he first arrived. Never in his life had he felt so insignificant and miserable. The image of Lorraine's betrayal was beyond his ability to understand.

Now, he questioned Lorraine's sincerity and truthfulness from the early days of their relationship. Her partner was a total stranger to him. The thought of having another man claim her as he had was a bitter pill to swallow, and he knew that for his own emotional well-being, he had to come to grips with it. The burning of the cabin was an act of rage, and since it took place he had not one pang of regret. The act had a cleansing value, but he was well aware that he was eliminating the stage where the event took place, and that had nothing to do with the reason for it happening in the first place.

Sitting against a tall white pine tree, staring across the miles of scattered cumulous clouds, Ken came to the conclusion that he should cut his furlough short and return to his crew. There was nothing to keep him here in Maine. His parents would understand his need to be with people who cared. He had always considered Lorraine to be his best friend as well as his lover and wife. "My God," he cried. "How wrong can a person be?" He never knew a day so long or a night so dark.

Moments after uttering the desperate cry, the darkness of the night was slowly displaced by a full moon that rose out of the eastern horizon to send soft shadows across the landscape. How peaceful it was to watch the world below from this perspective. He was already feeling the magic and was glad that he chose to come here. The flowering softness of an evening in June was comforting, yet it was a contradiction, for on the other side of the world he had just left, nations were tearing each other apart, desperately searching for easier ways to destroy their enemies. Here in the community where he grew up secure and happy, untouched by the ravages of war, he was stimulated by the solitude of the night, and felt a rush of tears, bursting for release.

It was natural that images of Lorraine flooded his thoughts at this spot. They had visited it often and sat beneath this very tree, listening to the whirr of the wind flowing through the canopies of the pine trees. Thoughts of her converted him to a quivering shell of a man, consumed by despair. Convulsive spasms of grief pierced his lips. He was unable to control the agony that was tearing him apart.

A slender figure appeared out of the dark shadows of the forest and hesitantly walked to his side, a witness to his grief. She kneeled beside him and gently placed her hand on his shoulder. He knew that touch; it was Lorraine. For years they had been so close they could often complete each other's sentences and read each other's thoughts without saying a word. At first the touch was like a caress capable of making all the pain go away. How he yearned for that touch again! But the reality of the moment consumed him and he angrily sloughed it off his shoulder.

"Don't you dare touch me," he cried, turning away from her.

She remained kneeling and told him, "The man you saw attacked me and threw me on the bed. You must believe that, Ken. I know how you must feel and I share your rage and torment, but it was not what your imagination portrays it to be. Your parents are worried about you, so I took a chance on finding you here."

"Go back where you belong. I don't need you anymore. I'm not completely in control of myself and may end up hurting you, so go," he warned her in a threatening voice.

"Don't you want to see Lori?" she replied.

"I did," he angrily snapped back. "That's what my surprise visit was all about... Now I even question if Lori is my child, so under the circumstances I think it best for me to not see her."

"How can you say that?" she cried, stunned with a loss of words to turn the situation around.

"You made it pretty easy, Lorraine. If someone would have told me that my wife could go to bed with someone else, I'd have beaten them to a pulp for insulting your character. Yet, with my own eyes I saw you like a common whore."

She began to protest and lost her voice, gasping for breath. She coughed uncontrollably and was on the verge of passing out.

Ken stood up and turned to look down on her. "I'm going back to my outfit in England. I'm just not in the mood to spend a lot of time trying to figure out what went wrong. Will you tell my parents that?"

She shook her head in the affirmative. "Yes, I'll tell them everything. I know that you burned the cabin..."

"That's correct. It was a therapeutic moment that salvaged my sanity. Right now I've lost my bearings, but I'll find a new way, and I can assure you that the future does not include you. That fact was a choice you made without my knowledge. Now I'm making a choice for myself." He completed the warning in a calm and objective voice that surprised him.

Lorraine, stunned by the anger and wrath of his response, stood up to face him. There was just enough light from the moon for her to see the rancor and contempt on his face.

"What about Lori?" she pleaded in desperation. "I don't blame you for your anger, but the act was not what it appeared. What about Lori? She deserves better from you... My God, Ken, give me a chance to explain... Don't let this sordid act become bigger than it already is. I beg you again, please... listen to me...." She began coughing again.

He saw the pain on her face and exclaimed in a high pitched voice, "The one time I really needed the comfort and grace of our love, you denied to me by an unspeakable act that made mush out of everything I held sacred. Right now I'm not capable of making any decisions about Lori... God, how I wanted to hold her in my arms and tell her how much she has meant to me, especially on those long, terrifying missions over Germany. I've held her picture close to my heart on every trip and prayed that I would survive so that she could have a chance to know who her Dad was..." He began to lose his composure, and, once again, tears of frustration dropped down on the rows of ribbons he wore on his uniform.

Lorraine knew her Ken. He was traumatized by the situation, and she prayed for a chance to take him into her arms so that she could overshadow all the pain that filled his heart. "Don't do this to me, Ken," she pleaded.

"It doesn't help, Lorraine," he replied. "I hate you for denying me the comfort and spiritual renewal I came home for... As for Lori, maybe, when this war is over, she and I will have a chance to get acquainted. Right now, I have a responsibility to my crew who need me, and I never realized how much I needed them until today." With that, Ken walked away toward the army sedan, leaving Lorraine motionless and filled with self-loathing.

He drove at top speed for two hours toward Grenier Field in Manchester, New Hampshire, where he turned the sedan back to motor pool and placed his name on the roster for the next available space on any plane going to England. The dispatch desk told him they were unsure of the exact time, but a transport was being loaded with supplies, and maybe he could find room on top of the cargo. He told them to set him down for it and that he would be waiting in the Officer's Club.

Grenier was an active airport with planes landing or taking off at a steady pace day and night. He ordered a ham and cheese sandwich and a cup of coffee to satisfy his hunger. He had not eaten for twenty-four hours. He was feeling guilty about leaving without seeing his mother and father and took a seat at the far end of the dining room so that he could write a letter to them before his plane took off, obtaining paper and pen from a nearby waitress station.

Dear Mom and Dad,

I'm sure that Lorraine has told you two what happened today. I was given a few days off. My Commanding Officer ordered me to come home and rest. Things have been difficult lately, and I also wanted to visit the home in Sanford, Maine, of one of my crewmen who was killed during our last mission.

When I arrived at the log cabin, unannounced, I found Lorraine in the bedroom with a stranger to me. I don't care to know who he is. If I did I'd probably do something foolish and kill him or injure him for life. It goes without saying that the scene triggered such deep hatred and a desire to do something, that I burned the cabin, and I'd do it again rather than leave it for her to be unfaithful behind my back. I can't put into words the hatred I feel for her right now, and that was the main reason I left in such a hurry.

I'm sorry I didn't get to see Lori. Her precious innocence sustains me and will continue to do so in the difficult days ahead. I love her with all my heart and soul. Would you tell her that for me?

I'll keep in touch, and please keep your letters coming. You have no idea how valuable news from home is to those of us away. You might tell Lorraine to never mind writing. I refuse to be a party to her duplicity. Whatever we had she completely and thoroughly trashed of her own free will, and I can't find it in my heart to give her another chance to do it to me again.

Love to all,

Ken

While Ken was writing his letter, the Officer's Club began to fill so that most of the tables were full. He was surprised by two female officers who stood before him holding cups of coffee. "Excuse us, Captain. May we share your table?"

"Of course, please sit down. I didn't realize that so many would be here this late in the evening. I'm Captain Kenneth Morgan," he remarked, folding the letter and placing it in his tunic breast pocket.

The two lieutenants took seats opposite him. "We're sorry to barge in on you like this. I'm Lieutenant Charles and this is Lieutenant Gibson. We just came in from England and the plane was freezing, so we plan to thaw out with as much coffee as we can hold," Lieutenant Charles admitted to him.

He noted that they both wore silver wings, and quickly asked, "Are you two pilots?"

Lieutenant Gibson nodded in the affirmative with a mouthful of coffee. "Yes, we just delivered twenty P-47 Thunderbolt fighter planes to one of our bases in England."

"You crossed the Atlantic?" he asked in wonder.

"Well, Captain," Lieutenant Charles answered. "It would be difficult to deliver a plane to England without crossing the Atlantic. Don't you think a woman is capable?"

"Lea," scolded her companion. "I'm sure he did not mean that."

He was shocked by the rapid response to the casual remark he had made to be polite. "It was not my intention to imply any such thing, Lieutenant Charles. I was simply concerned for your safety in a combat zone, that's all. I apologize for my choice of words. It's been a long day."

"Apology accepted, Captain Morgan, and I apologize for being so defensive," Lieutenant Lea Charles smiled at him. "Officially we are members of the Civil Service, not a part of

26

the Army although we fly Army planes from the factories to all of the overseas bases. Our official title is Women's Auxiliary Ferrying Squadron – WAFS for short. We have women qualified to fly single or multi-engine aircraft. I'm also qualified to fly the B-17.

"Our training period is the same as yours. You may be pleased to learn that our flight instructor, a male pilot, told us that many of the women were faster to learn instrument flying and were smoother on the controls. I add that to validate our ability to fly any mission assigned to us, with the exception of combat. However, the fighters we fly to England are loaded to capacity with ammunition in case we have to defend ourselves."

"I had you confused for WACs," Ken replied, impressed with her description of their roles. "I'm sure glad to know that planes are becoming available for us. We desperately need all we can get. The Thunderbolt is a tough plane with tremendous firepower. The British Spitfire does a good job, but there are so few of them, and they can't go all the way into Germany with us."

"We'll soon be delivering the new bubble canopy Mustang. What a beautiful aircraft," Lieutenant Charles enthusiastically told him.

"How long have you been flying?" Ken asked casually.

"Martha and I met at flight school. I've flown some with my brother, who had a contract flying the mail between Philadelphia and Boston. The first time I flew with him, he let me take the controls. It gave me a feeling of euphoria and joy that I have never found anywhere else."

He watched her and smiled. She had the fire in her dark eyes, and he understood what she was talking about, it had been the same with him. "There's a short verse penned by John Magee, a courageous Royal Air Force pilot during the Battle of Britain, that rings true to those who have experienced its magic."

Martha innocently asked, "What does the poem say anyway?"

27

Lieutenant Charles quoted the lines in her soft, melodious voice:

"Up long delirious blue
I've topped the wind-swept heights with easy grace
Where never lark or even eagle flew,
And while with silent, lifting mind I've trod
The high un-trespassed sanctity of space,
Put out my hand, and touched the face of God."

Ken heard her recite the words he, too, knew by heart. It was as if he was listening to it for the first time, and it touched him. "There isn't a serious pilot out there that has not had the same feeling of liberation." For some reason he could not understand, Ken had felt reassured and the queasiness in his stomach disappeared. For a moment he had been freed of his earthly strife and lifted above the turmoil that filled his heart. Whatever it was, Magee's soothing words or their interpretation by a total stranger, he was not going to question the fact that he was suddenly given a clear message for the future. His decision to return to his crew was a correct one.

A loudspeaker announced that the plane to take the ferrying pilots back to Seattle was loading at the passenger ramp. Lieutenants Charles and Gibson hurriedly finished their sandwiches and got up to leave.

"Good luck to you both," Ken told them.

"It was nice meeting you, Captain," answered Lieutenant Gibson.

Lieutenant Charles turned to him with a winsome glance and said, "You take care over there, Captain Morgan."

He waved as they left the room. For a while he had forgotten his troubles. The two ladies with their zest for life had lifted his spirits in the short time they were together. Finishing his coffee, he left the Club and went outside to watch their plane take off. The loading ramp had just been removed, and the plane idled to takeoff position. Within seconds, the pilot shot down the runway and lifted off.

A couple of Havoc A-20s landed shortly after on the same runway, probably returning from an anti-submarine patrol in the Atlantic. Grenier Field was buzzing with activity. It was strange, considering the circumstances, but he was actually anxious to get back to his outfit in England. The feisty WAFS, with their "can-do" attitudes had helped make him realize that he was not the only one fighting a war.

A few hours later, Ken was able to catch a flight to London on a DC-3 loaded with cases of C-Rations. The crew gave him a rolled up bunch of packing blankets so that he could stretch out on top of the cargo. The co-pilot had joked that he had plenty to eat on the trip, breaking into a carton of biscuits and chocolate. Ken then covered up and slept like a baby all the way across the Atlantic with the hum of the engines lulling him to sleep.

Within a week after his return to base, Ken was back in the normal routines of briefing for a mission, flying the mission, debriefing after a mission and, finally, crashing for a welcome night's sleep only to wake up and repeat the routine all over again. Overcast days were a welcome reprieve to the strain. The emotional roller coaster ride was difficult to handle. Everyone in the squadron shared the extreme pressure of the relentless pounding of Fortress Europe, regardless of the high attrition rate among them.

He had been given a newly rebuilt B-17 Flying Fortress with a crew containing three men that had previously served with him; the others were directly from the replacement pool. He spent all of his spare time with the crew, and they developed into a crack outfit with few personality conflicts. He had stressed five points which defined their purpose and contribution to the war effort: Their purpose is to destroy the German war machine, the economy which feeds it, the morale which sustains it, the supplies which nourish it and the hope of victory which inspires it.

Once their goals were accomplished, they will have won. He threw himself into each mission with a zeal which he knew was nothing but an escape mechanism to handle his inner turmoil. Three months after his furlough home, Ken had received over forty letters from Lorraine. All of them remained unopened. He punished himself hoping that it would, in turn, be even more insulting to her. He blindly placed each one in a shoe box and sent them back to her. It was his way of telling her that what they once had was finished. He even removed his wedding band and taped it to one of the letters. It was a desperate act that showed his resolve.

The only letters he opened were those from his parents. They had kept him informed of Lorraine's activities and how Lori was doing. Loraine had moved into an apartment close to the school so that she could walk; the scarcity of gas severely affected everyone's lives. They also sent him a few pictures of Lori. One of the last letters his mother had written contained a discussion of what took place when he came home:

Dear Son,

The news on the radio is not very encouraging, and we are all afraid that this ugly war is going to be long and costly. Our prayers are always with you. We just had word that Joey Salmon from your class was lost at sea when his Coast Guard cutter was torpedoed in the North Atlantic. As you know, his mother and I have been close friends for years. She's destitute with grief. The collective grief of the nation is measured by sorrowful mothers who had to say "good-bye" to their beloved sons for the last time. God only knows when it will end!

Your father wanted me to tell you that we see Lorraine and little Lori every week. She vowed to us that she has never been unfaithful to you, and told us what took place, and we accept her version as factual. According to her, you entered the room and saw the two of them scuffling on the bed together. The man had been there to repair the oil furnace in the cellar and struck up a conversation with Lorraine who, as you well know, is a lovely lady. After making a repair in the cellar, he came upstairs and asked her to check all of the heat registers in the house. When she went into the bedroom to see if heat was coming from the register in that room, he followed her and began to maneuver her towards the bed. She tried to stop him, but he was so aroused that he threw her on the bed and held her there, ripping her blouse. That's when you saw them. She reported it to the police, and they have arrested him.

She swears that she did not lead the man on or hint that he could take such liberties. We hope that this puts some of your rage to rest. She's a wonderful mother to your daughter, and your father and I love her dearly. Don't discard her for what you perceive took place. She deserves better than what you are doing to her right now. She's not handling this episode very well. The last time we saw her she looked exhausted.

We pray that this letter has helped to fill your heart with hope instead of hatred.

All our love

Mom and Dad

His reply had been short and to the point. He had no qualms about torching the cabin on the basis of what he saw with his own eyes. He told them that he saw the bedroom scene situation differently. He heard no screams of protest, which convinced him that it was consensual. So, the best thing for him to do was to continue the way things were going. It worked for him, right or wrong. In his heart, he believed that Lorraine had hoodwinked his parents, and dismissed their plea for forgiveness.

One day after a difficult mission that had cost him the lives of two of his crew, Ken was called into the squadron commander's office. Colonel Stan Knowlton was a red head with freckles around his nose and a smile usually on his lips. Ruggedly built, with a tendency to be pugnacious when his

Irish temper was aroused, the Colonel was a lover of straight talk and eyeballed Ken as he walked into the office. "Come in, Ken, take a seat."

"Thanks, Colonel," Ken was dead tired and slumped in the chair offered.

"I know that you're beat and have yet to go through debriefing, Ken, but I wanted to ask you something that will improve our chances of carrying out our assigned missions with fewer losses. We just can't sustain the losses we're now taking. Higher headquarters has come up with a plan to use a single plane as a pathfinder for the squadron. That is, they'll proceed the main formation by twenty minutes or so and drop incendiary bombs on the target. That will give the formation a greater degree of accuracy. Could I count on you being the first guinea pig?"

Ken was not enthusiastic about the tactic and replied with a frown, "The pathfinder is in a vulnerable position without flank protection that the box formation provides. Losses may even be higher."

"I'm aware of that, Captain."

"My navigator and bombardier are two of the squadron's best," Ken claimed. "Okay Colonel, I'll take the job."

"I was hoping you'd say that. I'm going to give you two of our new P-47s for escort all the way to the target and return."

Ken smiled at him. "I appreciate the offer, Colonel. Thank God for those ladies who deliver the planes. I recently talked with a couple of them at Grenier Field. They're quite a bunch."

"I wasn't very favorable to the idea until I was over at the fighter strip when they came in for a delivery, and I was impressed with their precision and discipline. They sure knew how to fly those fighters. If they were allowed to do combat, I would bet that they would be as aggressive as our male pilots."

"I have no doubt, Colonel."

"I know you're tired, Ken. Go through your debriefing and I'll see to it that your plane is outfitted for the morning."

"Thanks, Sir."

Chapter Four

The pathfinder mission worked very well. The incendiary bombs filled the cargo area. The navigator had more detailed maps than was usually provided to the bombers. Just prior to leaving the English Channel, two shiny new Thunderbolts appeared on each side of "Sweet Lori".

"Mad Dog One to Sweet Lori, do you read me?"

"This is Sweet Lori. We're glad to have you along for the ride."

"Happy to oblige. We've got extra fuel in detachable tanks we can drop when empty. That way we'll be able to ride shotgun for you to the target and back to the Channel. We'll position about one thousand feet to each side of you and two thousand feet higher so that we can attack any intruder of our air space. Good luck, Sweet Lori."

"Thanks, Mad Dog, over and out."

The presence of fighter escort had helped to keep the German fighters at a distance, which boosted the hopes of each member of the crew. However, the amount of flak thrown at the pathfinder was unbelievably heavy and was sustained for a long distance to the target area, an airplane manufacturing facility. It was necessary that they be as accurate as possible if the follow-on formation was going to be successful. It was almost as if the Germans knew what plant they intended to bomb and had placed all of their antiaircraft weaponry along that line of approach.

Twice the rugged fortress shuddered from direct hits. One was slightly behind the pilot's seat, sending shrapnel into the back of the seat, hitting Ken's left shoulder, and into his neck, opening wounds that bled freely. He was hurt but it was not a serious wound. He refused aid until they had completed their run on the target and the bombs were dropped. Shortly after they had climbed to a higher elevation and reversed course, he temporarily turned the aircraft over to his co-pilot, Jim Reams.

The radioman and the bombardier both helped to bind up Ken's wounds with compress bandages and gauze. Twenty minutes later they saw the main formation below and off to their right. Ken was pleased with the performance of the crew and congratulated them. His wounds were painful, but he was managing it. The part that bothered him the most was that he had been steadily getting weaker and weaker and had trouble focusing on the instruments, and passed out. Jim Reams took over while the rest of the crew pulled Ken out of his seat. Blood had been running out of wounds they had missed. Laying him on the floor behind the seat, they were horrified by an open wound in his lower back that still had a piece of shrapnel protruding from it. They sprinkled a liberal amount of sulfur powder on the wound and wrapped him up in several compress bandages, making sure to lay him on his side so that they could administer water and lukewarm coffee from the thermos bottles to help him replace the blood he had lost.

The co-pilot brought them back to base without further incident. Ken was removed to the infirmary and shortly taken by ambulance a few miles to the fighter plane airfield which had a hospital. They surgically removed the metal shrapnel from his lower back, cleaning and dressing all of his wounds. He had been lucky; there were no broken bones.

The next day, his crew came over to see how he was doing. The designated target for the day was overcast, so the crew took advantage of it by visiting the fighter base which had a better equipped Officer's Club and Enlisted Men's Club, and the luxury of a large Post Exchange. The hospital ward had only two patients at the time, Ken and an airman in traction at the far end of the ward with a broken leg.

Ken's crew told him that the latest scuttlebutt was that a flight of P-51 Mustangs with the new bubble top canopies was on its way to the field. The new planes were slightly more powerful than the earlier ones and had extended range capacity. Now they could have more fighter protection for their deeper penetration raids. An orderly opened the door to the Quonset hut to announce: "The flight of new planes have made landfall and are within minutes of touching down."

Several left the ward to view the spectacle of brand new Mustangs arriving in the theater. Jim Reams moved Ken's bed around so that he could see the field. Out of the western sky powerful silver Mustangs began to approach the landing strip in a precise formation.

"My God, their cutting it kind of close," he remarked, admiring the soft landings and precision of the pilots as a team.

One plane came in to buzz the runway and then made a steep climb pulling hard to the starboard. Ken and Jim instantly saw the reason - the plane had only one wheel in locked position. They both knew that sometimes erratic maneuvers can shake one loose but the chances were small. Evidently the pilot was trying to correct the situation and began a series of perfect barrel rolls and steep climbs, falling off in a high speed dive that ended only feet from the ground.

"Wow, I call that some precision flying," Jim announced. "So far, the wheel is still lodged in the housing. That pilot has got some tough choices to make."

Ken shook his head and tried to imagine what the pilot was going through. Suddenly he had a frightening feeling that it might have been one of the women ferrying pilots he had met at Grenier. This one was exhibiting a degree of excellence few pilots achieve. He was convinced that it was most likely the lovely Lieutenant Charles, and he prayed for a safe landing of some kind. Nineteen planes had landed, leaving only the one above the field going through every contortion a plane is capable of executing. The powerful engines screamed and roared with every set of eyes on the field glued on the wounded Mustang.

After several minutes of abrupt maneuvers, the pilot came down low at a speed slightly above a stall speed to survey the cement landing strip and the grass-covered field of half-grown corn beside it. She had radioed the tower of her intentions to come in on one wheel in the corn field and to have recovery vehicles nearby. The order was given, and several emergency vehicles lined up on the edge of the field.

The pilot headed away from the strip at full speed and made a tight turn slightly above the ground, lining up on a stretch of the corn field parallel to the emergency vehicles and began her descent. The single wheel was only inches above the ground when the pilot cut the engine and allowed the tail to touch down first, then she kicked the flaps upward on the side with the wheel in position to stabilize the forward momentum and dropped the flaps on the other side to give the plane some lift and some braking effort. For several feet the plane teetered on one wheel with the pilot applying the brakes so that it locked the wheel, allowing it to drag a furrow in the ground. Then the right wing dropped and dug into the soft earth pivoting the aircraft sharply to the right before coming to a stop. Ground crews were on top of the craft before it stopped completely.

"That was some performance," whistled Jim Reams. "Whoever the pilot is has got nerves of steel and skill that surpasses mine."

Ken remained quiet. It was the kind of performance he would have expected from a pilot who could quote Magee. He leaned back on his pillow and remembered how she had said good-bye. She was not an easy woman to forget, and Ken did not deceive himself that he had been attracted to her at first sight. She was the kind of person you could know for a lifetime and still discover new things about her. It was not fascination or infatuation, which he associated with teenagers; it went deeper than that. He remembered her because he had seen some of the same pain in her eyes that he was experiencing, and that made them kindred spirits.

Soon orderlies and nurses were busy preparing a bed for the pilot in the corner of the room closest to the outside door where they had arranged curtains so as to insure privacy. The crew all said "so long" to Ken and left the hospital. He turned his head so that he could hear what was taking place behind the screens. The doctor had asked a question, and the patient answered that she was all right; she had banged her head against the canopy. Ken was right; it was Lea. He recognized her soft voice. The doctor told her that she had a slight concussion and they were going to keep her quiet for a while.

"You have won the acclaim of some of the sharpest pilots in England, Lieutenant Charles. Congratulations on averting a disaster with your flying skills. Now, what can we do for you?" the doctor had asked in a gentle tone.

"I'd love a cup of coffee, Doctor," she replied in a low voice.

"I'll see that a fresh pot is put on for you, Lieutenant. The nurse will help you get ready for the night in an army nightgown. You know army regulations."

"That will be fine, Doctor, thank you. I am tired."

That voice was Lieutenant Charles! Ken smiled at his intuitive feelings. He asked the nurse to crank his bed so that he could sit up. The faint aroma of coffee smelled good to him, and he asked for a cup, asking about the new patient in a whisper.

"She's going to rest without any sedatives for the night. She suffered a mild concussion, and we'll monitor her condition throughout the night. The doctor thought that she will be fine in the morning. She was knocked out in the cockpit," the nurse told him. "Right now she's enjoying a toast and coffee, would you like that?"

"I would, thank you. Would I be out of order if I spoke to her?"

"Not at all. We're not that formal here in the field hospitals, and the ward is almost empty, so you won't disturb anyone, Captain."

She returned shortly with his coffee and a piece of toast with orange marmalade. The British do like their marmalade, he thought. Trying the coffee, he lifted his voice to speak to Lieutenant Charles. "Is this coffee as good as the one you had at Grenier Field in New Hampshire a few months ago, Lieutenant?"

"To be honest," she replied in that soft voice he remembered. "It doesn't quite measure up, but it does taste

37

good. I remember our short visit at the Officer's Club, Captain Morgan, isn't it?"

"Yes, I couldn't help hearing you talking to the doctor. Your voice is as distinctive as your flying skills. I salute you, Ma'am. You didn't learn to fly like that in the short time you've been in the WAFS."

"Thank you, Captain," she blushed at his praise. "I learned to fly as a young girl with my older brother who flew for a contract company to carry the mail. He's over here somewhere in England with Bomber Command."

"What's his name?"

"Captain Donovan Pool. Everyone calls him Don."

"The nurse told me that you need rest so I'll can the conversation for now. I'll see you in the morning, maybe have breakfast together," Ken suggested casually.

"That will be fine. We had only met for a few minutes in New Hampshire, but in this fast-paced war, that qualifies us as old friends. What are you in the hospital for, Captain?"

"A few shrapnel pieces hit me on our latest raid. I was cut up some, but will be fine in a few days."

"I'm glad, Captain. I am a little tired."

"Rest well, Lieutenant."

Mornings at an advance airfield in England during the war years started way before dawn, when fighter planes began to warm up in preparation for the day's work ahead. They were able to fly longer distances now, and that resulted in fewer casualties among the bomber groups who had previously had to slug it out all the way to Germany and on the return trip to the Channel without fighter protection. By that time, most of the bombers were pretty well shot up with casualties mounting to thirty percent. It placed a heavy burden on the morale of those who continued to knock out the ability of the Germans to wage war. The practice was almost a guarantee that few were going to survive the slaughter, yet they continued to carry out their mission with skill and sheer guts, regardless of the high costs.

For two hours the squadrons stationed at the field filled the air with screaming engines at full power as the heavily loaded craft struggled to become airborne. A small number had to abort. Ken observed the ground crews working on several that didn't make it. When he was brought to the hospital, all he had for clothing was his flight suit. Jim Reams brought him a pair of coveralls. The flight suit had been cut to pieces not by shrapnel but by the nurses and doctor who treated him.

He was still feeling a little weak. The smell of fresh coffee perked him up enough that he asked the nurse if he could get out of bed to eat a light breakfast. She agreed with his request, telling him it was good for him to exercise. She helped him to a small table at the end of the Quonset building. Oatmeal, toast and marmalade, and coffee were on the menu. He wasn't thrilled with the oatmeal, but he was hungry, and it did taste good to him. He saw Lieutenant Charles step out from her enclosed stall and walk towards the table. She was still wearing her coveralls.

"Good morning, Lieutenant," he greeted her.

"Good morning, Captain. The coffee made me get up. I woke when the planes were taking off and fell back to sleep for a while. I must have been tired. My headache is finally gone."

"That's good news," he replied, pushing the cream and sugar to her place at the table. He watched her carefully. She was of average weight and height with a soft, gentle manner about her that had a hint of self-consciousness, even bashfulness. It was a becoming attribute in contrast to the spirited defense of female fliers she was capable of mounting. He smiled at her. "Now that we're a captive audience of the hospital staff, how about you calling me Ken or Kenneth, and I call you Lea, which is a pretty name for a pretty lady."

She blushed at the compliment and smiled. "For longtime friends that makes sense. Do I detect a Down East dialect? Maybe Maine?"

"Maine it is. I'm from a small town northwest of Portland. And where are you from, Lea?"

"I grew up in the Adirondack region of New York at a town on Lake George called Diamond Point. My family has

39

lived there for years. I'm a proud descendant of the Mohawks, one of the original Americans."

"After you've been over here for a while, you realize that one of the best ways to get acquainted with people is to ask them where they come from. Most everyone feels comfortable talking about their roots and their hometowns, even to strangers."

"Have you been with Bomber Command long?" she asked.

"My squadron was one of the first to land in England. I've had over twenty missions so far. We still haven't learned how to keep the losses down. The fighters you deliver are the answer to our prayers. They'll make a big difference."

Lea observed Ken. His deep-set eyes reflected the horror of too many bombing raids that push the bomber crews to their emotional limits. He had a way of looking at a person as if he was looking through them. Early in the war, the haunting stare became a trademark affliction which all combat veterans shared. Ken seemed to be searching for something just out of reach. She had remembered that he had that same sad look at Grenier Field when they first met, and she surmised that he was teetering on the edge of a breakdown.

"Our group of WAFS will be leaving on the next available plane to the states," Lea told him. "An absence of a few days makes me thankful to return back home. I can't imagine how much all of you over here must miss it. I understand what you said about people's homes; they hold special memories that we can tap into whenever the need is there."

Ken heard her talk, yet the only image he carried from home was his Lorraine with another man, and it was tearing him apart. Lea, in her innocence, spoke of home with love, compassion and longing. He didn't picture it that way and without any forewarning, his eyes moistened and tears began to run down his face.

She saw the effect her mention of home had on Ken and reached across the table to clasp his fidgeting hands in hers. "I'm so sorry, I meant no harm, Ken. As a friend, I can confide in you that there is nothing wrong in asking for help from someone capable of doing so. I speak with experience for having been there."

"I apologize for my reaction," he sputtered, embarrassed that he could not control himself in her presence. "Excuse me..." He got up from the table and climbed into his bed curling up in a fetal position. Tears wet the white pillow.

She called for a doctor and told him about Ken's reaction. He was not surprised. Something had triggered a positive response that could be considered the first step at returning to normal. A little later, Lieutenant Jim Reams entered the ward carrying some shaving gear for Ken. Lea motioned him from the table.

"Good morning, Lieutenant. May I speak to you about Captain Morgan?"

Reams took a seat beside her and asked, "How may I help you, Lieutenant?" He was a tall, lanky South Dakota farmer with nerves of steel and a relaxed demeanor.

Lea told Jim about Ken's response to their conversation about home. "He seems to be extremely overwrought about something. This is only the second time I've met him, and both times he gave me the impression of being under a tremendous strain. I understand how grueling your bombing missions are, but his symptoms seem to go deeper than that. I'm simply a concerned friend."

"I appreciate your concern, Lieutenant Charles. In that, you are part of a very large group." Reams told her about Lew's death and his subsequent furlough home for a few days. He stressed that Ken returned to duty earlier than he had to, and that made everyone suspicious that something went wrong on the home front. He also explained that Ken always shared parts of his letters from home with the crew, especially those about his daughter, Lori. The crew named their plane "Sweet Lori" after her. Since his return to duty he has not said one word about life back home. "I haven't violated any confidences by telling you these things, Lieutenant. He's a far cry from the commander he used to be. All of his friends, and he has a large number, are concerned for him."

"I'm glad we've had this conversation, Lieutenant Reams. By the way, my brother, Captain Donovan Pool, is in the theater somewhere. If you happen to see him, tell him that his baby sister is thinking of him."

"I know Captain Don Pool. I was his co-pilot on a flight just before I was transferred to Ken's squadron. I'll be glad to pass it on when I see him. Well, Lieutenant Charles, it's been nice talking to you. Your display of talent yesterday made me feel like a rank amateur," Jim smiled, shaking her hand.

"Thanks. I may be gone by the time he wakes up. Would you say good-bye to Captain Morgan for me?"

"It'll be my pleasure. May Lady Luck always be with you, Ma'am."

Quietly placing the shaving kit on Ken's bed stand, Reams saw that he was sleeping soundly and left the ward to speak to the surgeon about Ken's situation. They both agreed that he was, for the moment, incapable of handling the command of a Flying Fortress.

Later that same morning, Lea was told to get ready to leave; a plane was warming up on the runway to transport the WAFS back to the states. She quickly combed her hair and slowly approached Ken's bed. He was still sleeping like a little boy curled into a fetal position. So young and so vulnerable to have seen so much, she thought.

The Flight Surgeon exercised his ultimate authority when he ordered the evacuation of Captain Morgan to a stateside army hospital at Boston. His decision was made quickly, and a space was made available on a returning B-26 two engine bomber converted to carry the sick and injured. The location of the hospital was within reasonable travel distance from his home in Maine. It was expected that his recuperation would be quicker and more complete in familiar surroundings away from the intimidating atmosphere of the world at war.

Ken was going through an extreme depression which drained him of energy and the will to survive. He was simply going through the daily motions and patterns of eating, sleeping, and remembering the horror of the war. He needed to be reassured that he was worth something, and that he was capable of contributing to that life. He was lost in a sea of morbidity that was consuming him. Nothing seemed to matter.

He still thought about Lorraine, even though he no longer carried blind rage in his heart. He slept a lot and felt himself getting weaker by the day. As time went on without improvement, he was afraid of wasting away to an insignificant dull idiot who mumbled when he talked and shuffled when he walked. That image frightened him more than anything else.

Chapter Five

Occasional flights of detachment and exaggerated awareness of things around him made Ken feel like a spectator instead of a participant in his own life. He sat up in his bed contemplating his condition. The more he analyzed himself, the more frightened he became. His condition had worsened since he came to Boston. He overreacted to normal, everyday incidents such as the banging of a door or the backfire from an automobile, which would send him scurrying for cover under the sheets.

The doctors had thought the familiar surroundings would solve that problem, but it had little effect. Something was holding him bondage. The first visit from his mother and father and little Lori was inconclusive. Of course he was glad to see them, yet when he held his daughter, he began to break down. Convulsive sobs scared the little one-year-old. The three left, concerned for his sanity. Their visit should have solicited a positive response from him, but it made him retreat to some dark, frightful corner of his soul that even frightened him while it was taking place. His delusions of inadequacy were completely out of character.

One day Ken opened a letter with no return address and read:

November 10, 1942

Dear Ken,

Your mother and father have informed me that you have been sent home to the Boston Army hospital. I have no way of appreciating your

44

courageous sacrifices, because you never write or call me.

I want to tell you that I have never stopped loving you, and that you are always in my thoughts and prayers, especially my prayers. I understand how the image you saw of me in the bedroom must have hurt you, but it is diabolically false – it never happened. If you will recall when you stepped into the room, we were both fully clothed with the exception of my torn blouse, which the pig had forcibly ripped. I've had the man arrested and he should no longer be a factor in our lives. Your perception has become reality in your eyes, and you are just plain wrong, dear Ken.

I want your happiness perhaps more than you do yourself, but I am not going to go through the rest of my life with a dark cloud over my head when I've done nothing to warrant such distrust. It really is up to you if you want to pick up the pieces of our marriage and put them back together again.

At some point in your life, you've got to recognize and share some responsibility for the disruption that's taken place. If it is in your heart to go forward, then give me some indication of your plans and dreams for the future. I'm not coming to Boston to see you until you have answered the question of where do we go from here?

If things stay the way they are now, and you continue to ignore me, it would be difficult. I'd have a hard time with that. You have no idea what your silence and denial of my existence has done to us. I do not want to be a complication in your life, and at the same time, I am not going to put myself in the position where you can ignore me again and distrust my actions. I just do not have the strength to fight you and I leave the next move up to you. Please believe me, I wish you well in everything, for I've never stopped loving you, never, never...

Do not be angered by the tone of this letter – look upon it as the end of an era and the birth of a new life instead of its demise.

Lori will come with your parents. They have been such wonderful supporters of me and Lori these past few months. Acknowledge their concern for our marriage, for it is real. Rest well my love, and try to rediscover that kind and gentle man I fell in love with many years ago and was so proud to marry. Don't you really want that ring back???

Love,

Lorraine

A few days before Thanksgiving Day, a group of amateur musicians, singers and comics came to the hospital to entertain the patients. Communities in which the hospitals were located were frequently organizing things to help the wounded take their mind off the war and their own suffering. There was a tendency to make the entertainment on the light side. The evening of the performance, Ken walked into the large recreation hall which had a small elevated stage at the far end of the room. He took a seat in the front row off to the left.

Some of the musicians were busy tuning their instruments and arranging the stage. Ken grew up in a home full of music. His mother was a beautiful piano player who sat for hours playing a large assortment of music from plaintive western ballads to Chopin's Polonaise. Even as a young man, music was capable of filling him with a spiritually rich experience of euphoria, and that sensation had been missing from his life since the war began.

Slowly the hall filled up with the walking wounded like Ken and the ambulatory patients in wheel chairs scattered around the seating area. The lights were dimmed in the hall while they were amplified on the stage flooding it with light.

A small orchestra of two violins, a clarinet and a piano player opened the evening with a rousting rendition of the Beer Barrel Polka. It was a favorite and the audience joined in singing the verses with a quartet composed of patients in the hospital.

A few of their friends and buddies in the audience hollered and called out to them. It was a grand beginning that united the audience with those on the stage. A medley of popular songs was played by the small ensemble and each performed as a solo. Ken was feeling good. The hall was filled with music and it lifted the spirits of all who were present, patients and performers alike.

A juggler dressed as a clown went through his intricate routine with five bowling pins. Everyone was waiting for him to drop one, and when he did, the crowd went wild, but he had fooled them, for the pin was made of rubber and bounced from the floor right back up into his mechanical-like hands, bringing a loud round of applause from the audience. The next performer was also a patient who dressed in a cowboy suit with a large hat pulled down to his ears. He and Ken had become friends. He played the guitar and sang several western ballads in a clear baritone voice. His first piece was *Don't Fence Me In* which brought the hall to their feet with whistles and claps. For an encore he did a medley of western songs: *Tumbling Tumbleweeds, Red River Valley, Cool Water,* and *Cowboy's Lament.* He was a crowd favorite and bowed to them losing his hat in the process. The hall erupted in more whistles and hollers of good fun.

The evening was going well for Ken and the audience. The sound of laughter and good-natured jostling lifted them from the trauma of the war and their injuries. An hour into the entertainment, the master of ceremonies, a well-known physical therapist from the hospital, walked on stage to the microphone.

"This evening, we're fortunate to have here with us an ensemble of talent who deserve a round of applause." The audience obliged and showed their appreciation. "We were not sure if we would be able to have the next segment of our entertainment tonight, but schedules have permitted their appearance. Gentlemen, I'm proud to announce that three members of our Women's Auxiliary Ferrying Squadron have taken time from their busy schedule to be with us tonight. They call themselves the Three WAFS, and here they are."

Three women dressed in light pastel blue evening gowns walked onto the stage. Two were carrying violins. The third member of the trio stepping up to the microphone was a dark-haired lady Ken recognized - Lieutenant Lea Charles!

"We are so happy to be here tonight with you men at the Boston Army Hospital. We just returned from England where we delivered twenty brand new P-51 Mustang bubble canopy fighter planes, to help escort our bombers stationed in England. For the past year we've played for our servicemen wherever we had a chance, and it's with a great feeling of pride and appreciation of your sacrifices that we could be here tonight with our wounded soldiers."

Ken could tell that she was a little self-conscious and shy talking in front of the audience. She searched the audience in the front rows and suddenly, made eye contact with Ken. He held his hand up to her and she acknowledged it with a slight nod.

"Well, we came to play instead of talk. I hope you like our repertoire. The first selection goes back to the First World War. My father was the first to tell me about it. It's a poignant song about a soldier and his sweetheart. It was as popular with our doughboys as it was with the Germans." With that, she took a seat at the piano and adjusted the microphone so that she could sing into it.

She had a soft soprano voice that filled the hall, accompanying herself on the piano with strong, sensitive fingers that ran over the keyboard with ease. Ken listened for every word, for he too knew the song by heart:

> Underneath the lantern by the barrack gate,
> Darling I remember the way you used to wait.
> 'Twas there that you whispered tenderly,
> That you loved me, you'd always be,

My Lili of the lamplight,
My own Lili Marlene.

Time would come for roll call, time for us to part,
Darling, I'd caress you and press you to my heart.
And there 'neath that far off lantern light,
I'd hold you tight, we'd kiss goodnight,
My Lili of the lamplight,
My own Lili Marlene.

Without any further introductions, she began a series of songs that touched the hearts of everyone in the hall, including Ken. Two selections that evoked the most memories for him were, *White Cliffs of Dover* and *I'll be Seeing You In All the Old Familiar Places*. He thought they were the most heartwarming renditions he had ever heard. It was as if he was hearing them for the very first time. He watched Lea's every move, spellbound by her loveliness, noticing a moist film in her eyes. She closed them and continued singing and playing so as to not let the audience see her emotional response to the music.

That evening, a transformation was taking place within his body that puzzled him. The fatigue and weariness that had taken over his body was vanishing under the spell of the music. The exultation of once again experiencing joy and poignant memories in his life was a miracle he did not understand completely until he continued to watch Lea with her gentle presence, filling the hall with her piano playing or her singing. Her spiritual involvement was also present, and Ken fervently believed that she was the one responsible for his sudden release from the terror that had been gripping him tighter and tighter over the past few weeks. He had given up on life. Now he was willing, even anxious, to know what it was like to again experience the exquisite joy of loving someone, and that someone was Lea Charles!

His admission of love was probably reciprocated by every soldier in the hall. It was transference on a large scale - common in army hospitals. The musical trio ended their performance with instrumental renditions of *September Song, Black Magic, Harbor Lights, Blue Moon,* and *The Whiffenpoof Song.*

At the end, Lea stood up with the two violin playing pilots and bowed to the audience. Their contribution to the evening's entertainment was a more subdued and sobering experience than what had preceded them. They had allowed the audience to feel and savor the pathos and joys that each selection was capable of evoking, and it lifted the spirits of the soldiers. Their ability to accomplish that was a signature of their skills as musicians, and the audience was consciously or unconsciously paying homage to that which defined the three pilots.

Ken crowded to the edge of the stage clapping his hands. Lea closed the microphone and kneeled down to speak to him. "Hello, stranger," she said.

Ken was more excited than he had ever been and was self-conscious to be dressed in his pajamas and army bathrobe. "You were wonderful tonight. You have the voice of an angel and succeeded in giving each and every one of us a respite from our problems. I'm at a loss for words, but I must say that you are very beautiful in that blue gown."

"I heard that you had been sent to Boston. We just got back from England. How are things going for you, Ken?"

The throng of soldiers pressing around Lea, asking her questions and complimenting her, made it impossible for Ken to give her an answer.

She leaned over to him and whispered in his ear, "I'll see you tomorrow. We're scheduled for another flight from Seattle."

He shook his head in the affirmative and left the crowded hall, a different man. In his heart, he contributed his transformation to the lovely dark-haired Lea with her ready smile and positive attitude. Ken had spent the evening analyzing her closely, and came to the conclusion that she was covering up a profound sadness that showed on her face and in her eyes. He recognized those symptoms and could even feel it when a breath of despair filled her heart. It takes someone who's been there to recognize the signs, and he was a charter member of the depression club. Lea was carrying a lot more heartache than she let on!

That evening, the nurse made her rounds to take Ken's vital statistics. His pulse, blood pressure and temperature were all normal, much lower than the previous readings the night before. The nurse also noted on the chart that Ken was more alert and motivated. She discussed his menu for the next day, going over the choices available. He selected a more varied and hearty selection than usual. It was in contrast to the fact that, previously, he had the nurse make the selections for him. She noted the changes in his general disposition and asked, "Is there anything I can get for you, Captain?"

"You know," he looked up at her and smiled. "I've been smelling that fresh pot of coffee you did at the nurse station. May I please have a cup?"

"You sure can," she replied. "If I found a piece of apple pie would you be interested to go with your coffee?"

"That would be nice, thank you."

Ken knew that something dramatic had changed in him in the past twenty-four hours, and he pondered that fact. He felt better than he had for a long time and attributed it to the prospect of seeing Lea again. It was a pleasant possibility to look forward to. He was well enough to feel some guilt about his feelings toward Lea. He was not now, and had never been, a fickle man who felt attractions to anyone except his wife. For months he had been under the illusion that Lorraine had broken their vows to each other, and the perceived act released him from his responsibility. As a matter of a fact, the first time he met Lea he tried to imagine her in that same light and concluded that she would certainly hold true to her vows, but then, he had thought the same thing about Lorraine, too.

The letter he received from Lorraine had an indifferent tone to it that made him uncomfortable as if he alone was responsible for the predicament they were in. It alarmed him and made him angry. He still believed what he saw; yet, she claims it was not so. The dilemma remained unsolved in his mind. In this time of weakness on his part, Lea had entered his life, and he could not shake the attraction he held for her, and he had no idea if his feelings were reciprocated.

How far he intended to carry his infatuation was a question he puzzled over for the rest of the night, resolving nothing. In the morning, he eagerly jumped out of bed and took a shower in anticipation of seeing Lea one more time. It dominated his thoughts and made him happy, a condition he had not experienced for a long time. The duty nurse and doctor heartily approved of his request to get dressed to leave the hospital for the day if necessary. They both thought it was a first step to his recovery. He knew that the Officer's Club was just around the corner from the hospital near the waterfront. He asked them to redirect Lieutenant Lea Charles to the Officer's Club.

It was just as if he had been liberated from a long confinement. He breathed deeply of the fresh sea air and thought of the City of Boston, which he had visited several times as a young man. He was always interested in American history, and Boston was where much of it took place. He noted a sign for Dorchester Heights and recalled that it was the place where the American militias had placed cannons dragged over the snow and ice from Fort Ticonderoga on Lake Champlain. Their overview of Boston and the harbor forced the British troops to evacuate the city, the first victory for the rebellious Americans.

The Officer's Club was busy night and day during the war. Ken selected a cup of coffee from the urn set up on the serving line and sought a table where he could wait for Lea. After a half hour wait, he harbored a nervous anxiety that she might not show up. Actually, he thought, in this time of such uncertainties, anything was plausible. The war had a way of setting its own timetable. It was a time of great national sacrifice that found its painful way into every household. Relationships were, at best, tentative and frequently shallow.

Ken was on his second cup of coffee when he saw Lea walk into the club and scan the people inside. She recognized him and made her way to his table. She was wearing her uniform and carried a purse strapped over her left shoulder, leaving her right arm free to return salutes.

"I was hoping you'd come, Lea," he exclaimed, holding a chair for her. "Can I get you a coffee or something?"

"A coffee will be fine, Ken. I ate breakfast earlier," she replied. Ken returned to the table with a cup and an insulated decanter of coffee and poured the two of them a fresh cup. Cream and sugar were on the table.

There were so many things he wanted to share with her that he didn't know where to begin. He decided to be bluntly honest, for the future was unpredictable for either of them. "Seeing and listening to you last night has helped to lift me out of my depression. Even the doctors and nurses are amazed at the change in such a short time. I must thank you for that." He looked into her eyes and continued, "How does a friend tell a friend that she's become an important part of his life?"

Lea heard the words he spoke and turned from his intense scrutiny. There was a nervous questioning look in her eyes. "I'm glad that you've improved, and if I have helped a fellow pilot who has carried more pain in his heart than is his share, then I'm thankful for the opportunity. What you say is true; we've only met for a very short period of time, and I can honestly say that under different circumstances maybe there would be a chance to get to know each other better, but this war has a habit of rearranging everybody's lives. Nobody knows that any better than I do."

"What do you mean, Lea?"

"I mean that we're still strangers, and to commit to a relationship can bring painful results. I lost a husband, an infantry captain, on Bataan eleven months ago, and I have a three-year-old son living in upper state New York with my parents."

"I'm so sorry, Lea. I never knew," he cried out to her, better understanding those times when he had seen intense pain and sorrow in her eyes. "I've been selfish thinking only of myself. Knowing this about your life makes me feel like a heel."

"Don't be too hard on yourself. Killed in action telegrams are going out to families all over this country at an alarming rate. Having told you that, I can truthfully say that there has been an attraction, some might call it chemistry, between us. I have not denied it, but there is danger in reading too much into it at this time in our lives. Wartime relationships frequently end in heartache. What do you say if we settle for friendship? Friends take care of each other and expect nothing in return. We're both committed to do our duty, and when the war is over, we can take a second look at where we are."

In his heart Ken knew that she was right. He clasped her hands between his and said, "You're correct in what you say. There is wisdom in waiting and being patient. I thank you for having the integrity and courage to say that. I will confess that I had fantasy thoughts of something different, but I was reaching beyond reality. Thanks for taking me out of the clouds to a safe landing. From that first time we met I knew there was something special about you. I will consider myself lucky for us to be friends."

She gave him a wistful smile and asked, "Do you have a picture of your daughter Lori?"

The question surprised him. "How did you know?"

"Your co-pilot, Jim Reams, told me in England that you had named your plane after her, *Sweet Lori*. I thought it was a wonderful gesture."

He reached for his wallet and pulled out two snapshots for her. One had a picture of Lori being held by Lorraine.

She studied the photos and passed them back to him. "You're a lucky man, Ken. Your daughter is beautiful, and you have a right to be proud of her. Your wife is also beautiful, Lori looks like her. You've never talked about her. I've sensed that something was wrong, but I have no intention of prying; that's between you and her and should remain so." She paused to select her words carefully. "Now, let me be crystal clear, Captain Kenneth Morgan. I am in no way, shape or manner interested in a ricochet relationship. I'm not saying that's what we have, but if it begins to take on that definition, then I'll drop it as quickly as it began. Your daughter, wife, and thousands just like them are the main reason we're fighting this war. Don't ever lose sight of that goal. They should be the single most important thing in your life."

Ken was getting a glimpse of the strong character and personality that made up this wonderful woman across the table from him. How sad her life must be. "You have a talent for getting to the heart of a matter, and I agree with you. I think I needed to have it spelled out to me. My mother and father tried a few days ago, but I wasn't ready to listen. I'm sorry about your husband; he must have been a very special man to have won your heart. I hope that I can be a worthy friend."

"I can't tell you how pleased I am that we've had this frank conversation," she smiled at him. "We both needed to mark out some boundaries. I'm due back at the airport shortly. The ferrying shuttles are being pressed to the limit to get the planes overseas. We'll soon be delivering planes into northern Africa. I want to get your mailing address so that we can write. I left my address with your duty nurse back at the hospital in case I missed you here at the Officer's Club."

"Thanks for that," he said, taking a small pad of paper from his tunic pocket and writing out his mailing address.

They continued talking as a civilian woman entered the dining hall and looked around the room. She was a slender woman dressed in a light green dress with a lace collar and a dark blue blazer. She wore a small green beret on the right side of her head at a rakish angle. Her light green eyes darted across the room, reflecting a nervous tension as if she was uncertain of herself. She walked directly to the table Lea and Ken occupied. There was a worried look on her face as she made eye contact with Ken.

He saw her from across the room and got the shock of his life. It was Lorraine.

Chapter Six

"Hello, Ken," Lorraine announced nervously.

Lea recognized her from the snapshot with Lori, and made up her mind it was time for her to leave as gracefully as possible.

"And you must be Lea, the nurse at the information desk mentioned. I'm Kenneth's wife, Lorraine."

"This is a surprise, Mrs. Morgan," Lea acknowledged her, getting up from the table. "I have a flight to catch and was about to leave. I wish you a speedy recovery, Captain Morgan. Your husband is a brave man, you must be proud of him, and I'm sure you two have much to talk about. It was nice meeting you, Mrs. Morgan."

Lorraine fought her jealous instincts and remained civil. There was something about Lea that quickly disarmed her anger. "Thank You, Lea."

Ken expected a blow out to take place and was relieved that a bad scene was avoided. He watched Lea leave the Officer's Club without saying good-bye to her and motioned Lorraine to a chair.

"Would you like some coffee?" he asked in a strained voice.

"Yes, but more than anything I simply want to talk with you, Ken. I did not come to create a scene or to judge you for what has taken place. If you're going to have coffee I'll have one with you, but to be honest, I'd rather take a walk outside so that we won't have to share our conversation with others."

"That suits me fine; it's a nice warm day for late November." He knew that she was nervous and uncomfortable. Her presence in Boston unannounced was significant, and now that they were together, he was prepared to settle their differences and get on with his life.

The club was beginning to fill up, and Ken and Lorraine threaded their way through the crowd coming in for lunch. Lorraine quietly followed him, saddened by his deep-set eyes and hollow stare. The Boston port area was a beehive of activity filled with boats of every description, loading and unloading cargo. He led the way to a bench near the commercial docks and motioned for her to sit down. He had been thinking about what he was going to say to her, but the suddenness of her appearance left him nervously searching for words.

"We can talk here. Where's Lori?"

"My sister Aline is caring for her at our apartment in town. I came to Boston on the train." She took a seat on the bench and confronted him. "Are you angry that I came?"

"No, it's just so unexpected," he replied, avoiding her penetrating stare.

"Tell me truthfully, Ken. Would you have left to go back to your squadron without seeing me again? Don't be afraid to express what's in your heart. This may be the most important conversation of our lives, so don't tarnish it with words that are not true." Her composure was slowly unraveling, and all she really wanted to do was take her lost husband in her arms and hold him.

She was lovelier than he remembered. Sitting beside her, he picked up the familiar essence of heliotrope she had used for years. He took a deep breath and turned to her, "There is a possibility that I might have, Lorraine. That's not to say that it would have been the right choice. To be honest, I haven't given much thought to anything. I've been sort of drifting and like these massive ships here at the port, was looking for a safe harbor."

"Has lieutenant Lea Charles had anything to do with your decision?" Lorraine asked in a shaky voice. Her presence bothered her, and she was anxious to know what was going on.

"Lea has been a good friend, really just an acquaintance, when I desperately needed one. She's a pilot and understood some of the things it's difficult to explain to those who've never flown. She also was sympathetic to my predicament because her husband was killed on Bataan."

"Did my latest letter make any difference in your thinking? Your mother and father have been so worried about you. They begged me to come alone to sort things out. I'm going to tell you one more time, Captain Morgan. I was never unfaithful to our vows with the man you yanked off the bed, or to anyone else, period. Now if you can't accept that, then we have no other place to go except our separate ways." She was on the verge of tears. She could not believe that she was talking to him this way.

"I understand what you're saying, Lorraine, but I keep thinking about that moment in the bedroom, and ask, over and over, why you couldn't tell me right then? It would have saved a lot of pain. Instead you simply cried and remained silent." It was a question he really wanted answered.

She looked at him with tears dimming her vision and explained, "I was in shock at that time. A part of me was afraid that you might kill the man, and he was not worth killing. I did try to reason with you at the lookout, but your anger rejected any attempt to explain. Your mind was made up and nothing could change it. I've felt so cheap and helpless that I could not be there for you in your time of need. I've always supported you, and I never stopped loving you..." Lorraine searched her blazer pockets for a handkerchief, blowing her nose and wiping the tears from her eyes. "I say it again, my dear Ken, I'm so sorry that this happened to us. Lori loves you, and I love you with all my heart. Please don't turn your back on us, especially Lori. She doesn't deserve your rejection."

"I never meant to hurt either of you, Lorraine. I came home because it was the only place I knew I could find the peace and comfort I needed. My head was all mixed up. I'd just had a bad experience losing my belly turret gunner when we had to bring our bomber home on only one wheel. The landing crushed him. It was the hardest thing I've had to deal with, and for a while, I was not myself. I requested permission to return to Maine; Lew was from Sanford. I visited with his parents and then headed straight home without contacting you. You know what happened after that."

It was the first time Lorraine had heard what had taken place previous to his visit. "I can't tell you how sorry I am, Ken. Can't we start over again and put this episode behind us?" she pleaded.

Ken looked deep into her tear-filled eyes and was thankful that she had made this trip. If she had not come to Boston, he probably would have been proud and pig-headed and left without settling anything. "I think we owe it to each other," he replied in a low voice.

"If you don't take me in your arms and kiss me, I'm going to scream!"

He didn't need to be asked a second time. They embraced there on the Boston waterfront, and memories of days past filled each of their hearts. The thrill of her soft lips sealed the pact they had just made to each other. They remained in a tight embrace for a long time, frightened of how close they had come to losing that which they had treasured for many years.

Ken held her at arms length and looked into her eyes. "You're lovelier than I remembered. Thank you for having the courage to come to Boston. Listen," he explained excitedly. "Why don't we head back to the hospital and see if I can get a pass to go home for a few days? I do want to see our daughter. I apologize for my impulsive behavior."

"The apartment is small, as you'll see, but it's cozy and comfortable near the school," she responded with a smile. "I've been so afraid that I had lost you. There seemed to be nothing I could do to change it. I poured my heart and soul out to you in those letters. When you returned them unopened, it really hurt."

He wrapped his arms around her again. "I can be stubborn at times. Forgive me. Can we rebuild the cabin?"

"I had a carpenter look at the place, and he told me it would be impossible to get the materials now that the war was on. I just recently received a check from the insurance company. I never told anyone you had torched it, and no one knew you had returned, so I kept quiet about it. I was sick when I saw the ruins. All of our personal items and pictures were gone in a flash. Thank God I had the Studebaker with me. The carpenter told me that he could sell the land with the well and septic system you installed for a lot more money than we had invested in the cabin and land combined, but we can talk about that later."

He had forgotten how resourceful and thorough she was about everything. He smiled at the business-like way she handled students in the classroom, knowing that she was a strict disciplinarian who exercised her authority with fairness and compassion. She had that knack of inspiring excellence in her students. At the end of the year when they were ready to pass on to another class, most of the students lamented leaving her.

"By the way, how is the Stude running?"

"I've had no problems with it since you left. Tires are difficult to find, but I don't drive much anyway. Right now I'm rationed to three gallons of gasoline a week, and that doesn't go very far. The Champion engine in the Studebaker is one of the most economical vehicles on the road."

"You're a great homemaker, Mrs. Morgan; I do love you. Come, let's check to see if we can go back to Maine."

They checked with the doctor on his floor who was enthusiastic at the prospect of his going home. It was, they knew, what he really needed. The doctors asked him to report back to them prior to his return to his unit so that they could ascertain his fitness to fly again. A few minutes later, Ken and Lorraine rushed to North Station to take the next Boston and Maine train. They were going home at last.

The old home town was much as he had left it. Many of the homes needed paint, but that was something that would be remedied as soon as the war was over. Everything was on hold until then. Almost every home proudly displayed the blue star framed in a red and white border indicating that a family member was serving in the armed forces. The presence of a gold star denoted the death of a family member. As the war dragged on more and more of the stars were exchanged for gold ones, shattering families and changing lives forever. The price for victory had been borne by the collective sorrow of grieving mothers whose sons were buried, forever young, in graves on foreign lands, fighting an enemy to free a people they hardly knew. The destructive war had wiped out, forever, the age of innocence Ken had known so well in his childhood.

At first, it was awkward in the small apartment. It made him feel even more guilty for torching the cabin. He and Lorraine had been in the apartment for a short time when her mother brought Lori home and knocked on the door. Lorraine asked Ken to answer it. He did so with some apprehension.

"Hello, Ken," his mother-in-law, Mrs. Carr, warmly greeted him with an embrace. "It's nice to have you home safe." She turned to pick up Lori and continued, "Your little daughter is anxious to see her daddy."

Ken reached out for Lori. She released her hold on her grandmother and wrapped her arms around his neck holding on tightly. How comforting it was to be loved by such a precious human being. He held her close and thanked God for the blessing. He remained silent for a few moments to savor the joy of holding her close to his heart. She released his neck and ran her tiny fingers over the Captain bars on his shoulder, and then fingered the rows of ribbons on his uniform.

"Daddy has wanted to do this for a long time, sweetheart," he whispered to her in a wavering voice.

Mrs. Carr excused herself. "I'm going to leave the three of you to yourselves."

"Thanks for everything, Mom," Ken said, turning to Lorraine with Lori still clinging to him.

"She loves you, Ken. Every night we say our prayers for your safety, and she kisses your picture before settling down for the night. We send our love to you on the stars. We're so thankful to have you here. Home is where the heart is."

"I feel so stupid about my rampage. I genuinely loved the cabin. I almost lost you and Lori and just about drove myself insane."

"You burned a house, not a home. Our home is here with all of us together in this room. It's not in a collection of boards and windows," she said, hugging the two most important people in her life.

That evening they pledged their love and fidelity to each other, bringing hope and promise to the future. Ken had spent three days at home visiting with family and friends. As good as it was, he felt something different in the town. In reality, their lives could never be complete until the war was over. It was a time of uncertainty, apprehension, even despair, but it was also a time when unity of purpose cemented the people together in the noble pursuit of peace for the world. Though he grew in the warm presence of his family, Ken remained committed to the important task at hand. Until that was finished, everything was temporary, which placed a stress on everybody's shoulders. Consequently, at the end of the furlough, he was ready to return to his squadron, and left with fresh memories of the ones he loved.

He had checked in with the Boston Army Hospital and received a clean bill of health from the staff. His orders were to proceed to Plattsburgh, New York, where he would be assigned to a brand new aircraft which he could ferry to England. He took a train west to Albany and then transferred to one enroute north to Montreal. He got off at the air field at Plattsburgh on the western shore of Lake Champlain where he reported to the officer of the day for instructions. He stayed overnight at the base's visiting officers' quarters and was told the following morning that he was assigned to ferry a P-51 Mustang or a Martin B-26 Marauder two engine attack bomber.

He complained that he had never flown either type of aircraft. He wasn't afraid of learning on the job, but a brand new aircraft was a lot of responsibility for a novice to assume. He asked if there was any person on the base with experience so that he could talk to them before he tried the controls. The

Officer of the Day sent him to the Officers' Club where a Lieutenant Gibson was eating breakfast. She had several hours on the P-51. Ken followed up on the suggestion and was directed to a table in the club filled with four WAFS; one was Lieutenant Martha Gibson. He remembered her from that first meeting at Grenier Field.

"Excuse me, Lieutenant Gibson," Ken introduced himself. "May I have a word with you?"

She turned to look who called for her and recognized him. "What can I do for you, Captain?"

"Do you remember we met once at Manchester, New Hampshire?"

"Yes, I was with Lea Charles," she replied.

"Well, the army wants me to return to England to report to my base. Since I'm a pilot, they must have figured I could bring one of our new planes over with me. I've flown hundreds of hours in a B-17, but I've never flown a P-51. Can you give me some pointers on its flight characteristics?"

"You came to the right place, Captain," said one of the WAFS. "We're prepared to leave soon with a flight of Mustangs. You can join our group. All four of us have made several trips to England without losing a single plane."

"Let me get a quick cup of coffee and a donut; then I want to hear what you pilots have to offer. I'll be proud to tag along with such an experienced bunch of pilots." He was in luck and rushed to the serving counter for coffee.

Lieutenant Gibson glanced at his overseas ribbons on his uniform. He wore among the service ribbons the Bronze Star, Distinguished Service Medal and a Purple Heart. "The privilege will be ours, Captain. We've been doing a regular shuttle run to England for several months. Soon, we'll be able to go as far as Algeria in Northern Africa after a refueling in England."

"The Mustangs and Thunderbolts you've been delivering have been a Godsend to us in the bombers. Even then our losses are high," he admitted soberly.

"We've often wondered if the heavy losses at Bomber Command are worth the effort. Of course, we have no way of gauging the results," said one of the WAFS.

It was a question he had often pondered himself. "My pay scale does not allow me to be privy to that kind of information. However, if Bomber Command continues to pursue the initial goals, then we must be making a strategic difference in Germany's ability to produce war machines. You may be interested in a true story I've been told by a respected observer."

"Please continue, Captain," they answered in unison.

"One of our bombers, a Liberator, returned from a flight over Germany badly shot up with several unexploded shells in the fuselage. When our armament specialists broke open the cartridges, they found several notes in Czech which said. 'This is all we can do for you now.' The cartridges were assembled without explosives which would have torn the bomber apart. There are a lot of brave people putting their lives on the line just like our soldiers. When the going gets tough, I think of those people and am inspired by their quiet courage."

The pilots talked a lot about the flight characteristics of the P-51. The WAFS all agreed that it was a very forgiving plane to control. Its maneuverability and speed were two features that a novice might underestimate because its speed was deceptive due to its slipperiness and its quiet engine. They assured him that once he had located the basic controls, he would be able to fly the aircraft with ease. Its sturdy construction and agility made it a fun plane to fly. Landings were generally faster than in the bombers even though the stall speed was about the same for both craft.

The group commander was a Major Allen. Ken accompanied Lieutenant Gibson and the others into a conference room where the plan for the delivery was discussed. They were to fly from Plattsburgh to a field in eastern Newfoundland where they would refuel and be loaded with a full supply of fifty caliber ammunition for the six machine guns in every plane. From Newfoundland they were to fly in a straight line for Anglia County in southeastern

England. They were to test their guns immediately after leaving Newfoundland and were to maintain radio silence on the second leg of their journey. The formation would be their normal arrowhead configuration with two tiers of aircraft and the point position was taken by the navigator who led the way.

Ken was supplied a full flying suit which he carried out to the planes. Lieutenant Gibson climbed up on the wing opposite Ken and pointed out the various control locations. He started the engine and taxied around an empty tarmac area while she stayed on the wing holding on to the cockpit handles. He was satisfied that he would be all right, surprised at the speed of the aircraft and the ease of the controls. She laughed and told him that it wasn't called a Mustang for nothing.

He was going to enjoy the experience and looked forward to the trip. Major Allen announced that they should take their assigned positions in the formation immediately after becoming airborne. The lead plane would hold the speed during this formative period to quarter throttle. She asked if there were any questions from the group. There were none. The major concluded: "I have one last announcement to make. We have the privilege of being accompanied by a veteran B-17 pilot who will occupy the slot at the center rear of the formation. On the radio frequency he will be known as 'Little Bo Peep.'"

Chapter Seven

"Little Bo Peep" – Ken couldn't suppress the smile that crossed his lips. The good-natured WAFS had given him the title in good fun and he accepted it in the same spirit. Even now, twenty years later, he could intimately recall that trip from Plattsburgh at the controls of a new Mustang. He fell in love with the aircraft. It was easy to fly, and even standing still on the runway it was a beautiful plane.

He took his place at the tail end of the formation at about 10,000 feet and relaxed to enjoy the New England scenery below. The Green Mountains of Vermont and the White Mountains of New Hampshire were magnificent from the sky. He had traveled in and around them on the ground, but he was seeing them for the first time from the air.

In all of the flying experience he had accumulated, he never saw a formation come together so smoothly and precisely as the WAFS had accomplished enroute to their first objective. They held their formation in a tighter cluster than he flew in Bomber Command, and it took only minimal directions from Major Allen, who rode on the starboard edge of the arrowhead. Ken continued to be impressed with their skill and discipline, even when they were chattering on the radio, which began soon after they had formed up.

The airbase in Newfoundland was heavily fogged in, so the ferrying command vectored the flight to Dow Field at Bangor, Maine. Crews were waiting to fill their fuel tanks and the ammunition supply for the six fifty-caliber machine guns in each plane. After a hurried stop for chow and restroom visits, they climbed back into the planes for the longest leg of their journey. By now, he had been accepted as one of the

66

group, and they went out of their way to treat him as if he had never flown before. They checked to remind him of the manifold settings and the fact that the cockpit canopy was securely fastened. Once they reminded him to double check the position of his landing gear lever. He smiled at the pampering attitude and told himself that never in his life had he had twenty women so protective of him at the same time. It felt good.

Every aspect of the flight was carried out with a flourish. Once they were in international waters, the planes were to peel off to the starboard and test-fired their weapons into the water, then reform at the proper altitude in the same sequence they had used after takeoff. Ken was the last to test his guns and fired a sustained burst while in a steep dive pulling up maintaining the firing. He was surprised at the flat trajectory of the machine guns and how quickly the gun's recoil slowed the aircraft. He knew from watching the Mustangs perform on several missions that they packed a heavy punch. His short burst gave him a welcome sense that he was not naked just in case an enemy plane spotted them. The women treated the firing exercise as a lark and put their planes through some acrobatic maneuvers before forming up. It eased the boredom.

The closer they got to the British Isles, the more sober their radio transmissions became, and once landfall was made, they disappeared completely. He could feel the tensions that seemed to permeate the formation. They had entered a combat zone, and everyone was alert. Soon a couple of British Spitfires appeared on each side of them. They were to act as guides to the airfield rather than using the radios to inform a potential enemy of their presence. They landed in the field closest to his squadron, and as soon as he reported with the other pilots to the receiving base, he made preparations to be transported. His good-bye was brief. He saluted and hugged every one of the pilots. His admiration had been won by their courage and skills. He was treated like a favorite mascot and kind of enjoyed it.

The base of operation for his squadron was drastically changed from the one he had left. The planes had been outfitted to a newer version of the B-17 with a chin turret in the nose. The greatest changes were the facilities for the crews. Better and larger barracks, mess rooms, recreation halls with movies available, and the usual ping pong tables and writing desks for those important letters home. The heat for the Quonset huts were centrally located coal stoves with a few using peat moss and wood. The population was larger with a permanent corps of replacements which took on temporary jobs until they were assigned to a crew.

Not only was the base updated with physical comfort facilities, the tempo of operations had picked up appreciably. Longer missions were executed on a daily basis using several squadrons in a solid formation. Fighters were plentiful in the theater, and they drew a large number for every flight of bombers. Their "little friends" were welcome and increased morale several notches.

The plane and crew assigned to Ken was one of the new Flying Fortresses. He was saddened to learn that his old co-pilot, Jim Reams, was killed on a raid shortly after Ken had gone on leave. "Sweet Lori II" had been lost at the same time over France. Most of the crew were able to exit the craft in time to parachute to safety. They were taken prisoners and ended up in a POW camp. At that time during the war, the POW crews were the responsibility of Luftwaffe personnel and they made an effort to abide by the Geneva Convention. They frequently notified the American high command the names of those in a POW camp and those who had been buried with full military honors. The American and British command reciprocated similar information to the Germans.

Ken's first order of business was to take a vote of the new crew members, three officers, and six enlisted men, about naming their plane "Sweet Lori III." He explained how much it meant to him and they voted unanimously. It was not simply a tribute to his daughter, it was also a way of honoring those who had flown and perished in the previous two aircraft. To the new crew they were strangers, but to Ken they still lived in his heart and in his dreams every night.

The belly gunner, Corporal Herman Ranta, a small-framed young Finn with blond hair and blue eyes, was a talented artist who volunteered to do the portrait of Lori on the plane's nose. It was a fortunate choice. The very young Corporal Ranta gave Lori's portrait an ethereal mystique that seemed alive and vibrant. Every person who saw the portrait was drawn to her eyes, which seemed to be looking at the viewer no matter the angle they approached the plane. Using one of Ken's most recent snapshots, Corporal Ranta began the work during a rainy spell under a tarpaulin.

Ken came to know the young man from Michigan while he was working on the painting. Ken made a point of frequently reminding the men that they were part of a team. Therefore he kept the demands of military protocol to a minimum. He stressed the availability of himself to discuss any issue at any time without the barrier of rank. His approach to crew integration gave him one of the most loyal and efficient crews in the squadron. The secret was simple. Respect for the crew came from the Captain down the chain of command. All the men knew it, felt it, and observed how he was always quick to defend them and take responsibility for their mutual effort. Once that fact became recognized, respect was returned. It was not his nature to be buddy-buddy with the men, but he was always approachable and genuinely friendly. He bore the responsibility of command with grace and confidence.

Their first bombing run after Ken's return to the squadron took place on January 1, 1943. Operation Torch, the invasion of North Africa, had started two months earlier. The plan for the mission was unique. They were ordered to fly into Germany to bomb their selected target, and then exit the country south through France and across the Mediterranean Sea to land in the Algerian desert, where airfields were rapidly being developed. Rumors had it that North Africa was going to be the springboard for the European continent. The route to return via Africa was slightly shorter and less hazardous than the one across the English Channel. It also gave them a chance to travel the route in reverse with another bomb run into Germany, then back to their command center in England.

The change in tactics was unsettling to the German higher command because they had already established heavy anti-aircraft protection to cover the most used routes to potential targets. This change kept the enemy on the defensive, never knowing for sure where they were coming from. The first trial run went well with only two planes lost. The presence of Mustangs and Thunderbolts riding herd on the lumbering bombers was a great source of comfort and pride. On any given flight, the Germans always lost more fighters than the Americans, a tribute to their skill and their sleek aircraft.

Once the formation landed in Algiers, they were instructed to remain with their planes and to sleep in them. Toilets in the form of slit trenches were provided the men close by their craft. A field kitchen had been established between the bombers and a parking area for fighters. That night the crews were chilled by the rapid heat loss that is typical of desert areas, and they gladly slept in their flight suits.

Ken's exhaustion was complete. Even the ribs on the fuselage floor did not bother him. His crew were still sleeping when he woke to the sound of an aircraft warming up close by. He quietly stepped outside, noting that the sun was already up. The heat of the day was beginning, and he shed his flight suit and boots. The plane was parked in a sea of sand as far as the eye could see. Off to their starboard a squadron of P-38 Lightnings were parked along the runway. It was the first time he had seen one up close. It was a large aircraft with two engines and two fuselages. There was a deadly look about it even when sitting still. It had a greater range than the Mustang or Thunderbolt.

Scanning the airfield complex, Ken saw the smoke coming from the field kitchen and walked over to see if they had any coffee. It had been twenty-four hours since he had eaten anything, and he was starved. The mess sergeant and his helpers were busy preparing for the morning rush. He inquired if he could grab a cup of coffee.

"The urn on the tailgate of the Dodge weapons carrier is all set, Captain; help yourself. I've got a fresh batch of cinnamon rolls you can start with." The mess sergeant placed a large tray beside the coffee urn.

"Thanks, Sergeant. Those P-38s are a great looking aircraft, aren't they?" Ken remarked, admiring them at this close distance.

"They sure are. You might not believe it but those fighters were flown in just minutes before your squadron landed here. We expected to see some hotshot pilots climb out of them, but you know what?"

"I bet they were women," Ken interrupted knowingly.

"You've got it, Captain. They knew how to fly those birds too. We were all surprised that the theater command would allow women to fly in an active war zone. I understand your squadron is going to make another run into Germany on your return trip to home base in England."

Ken was always surprised at the accuracy of the scuttlebutt that was active on every base. "That's my understanding, Sergeant. Your coffee and warm rolls are delicious. Have the ferrying pilots already left?"

"No, Sir. They're encamped in the portable officers' quarters at the rear of the planes. They should be here shortly. Our CO has got a DC-3 ready to transport them out of here as quickly as possible. Scrambled eggs, spam, and oatmeal is now available on the chow line, Captain."

"Thanks, but I'll stick to coffee and another roll." Ken helped himself and took a seat at one of the temporary mess tables set up in the open desert airfield adjacent to the field kitchen.

Ten minutes later, he saw the WAFS walking single file through the chow line. Ken curiously scanned them to see if he recognized anyone. As they drew closer, he saw Lea Charles, who seemed to be in charge of the group. They were all dressed in regulation army coveralls with fatigue caps. She selected her breakfast and turned to look for a suitable seat. Her eyes lit up when she recognized Ken watching her. By then, men from Ken's squadron were also lining up for breakfast.

"How nice it is to see a friendly face this far from home," she declared, placing her tray opposite him. "We watched your squadron coming in, and I recognized 'Sweet Lori.' How've you been, Captain? I hope everything is going well. How's your daughter?"

Ken thought she looked tired. "I'm doing okay, Lea. It's good to see you again. No matter where I go from New England to North Africa, I run into you and your pilots. How did you like that P-38 Lightning over there?"

"Oh my, that's a pilot's plane," she exclaimed excitedly. "It's an artillery platform with the heart of a racer. So far, it's my favorite."

He grinned at her enthusiasm. "It was what I'd expect you to say. I flew a Mustang from Boston to England with a group of WAFS. Lieutenant Gibson was with us."

"I haven't seen her in ages," Lea told him. "We had a little trouble on our way in yesterday, so this may be our last trip to North Africa."

"You mean German planes?" he asked with concern.

"Yes, they jumped us over the ocean. We maintained our formation and outran them."

"You shouldn't be in this theater, Lea. The brass must know that, too."

"Our commander volunteered us for the mission because of the desperate need for fighter aircraft in this zone. We all have to do the things we do best, it's not as if we were in a combat zone doing tactical flights," she explained.

He asked Lea a question that had been on his mind from the beginning. "If you were to be hit by German planes while making a delivery, what are your instructions?"

"To avoid action by any means possible. If there is no other way, we are allowed to defend ourselves. The planes are armed as you know. We've not been trained to do tactical maneuvers, but if my flight was threatened, I'll do whatever is necessary to remove that threat."

There was a flash of fire in the gray depths of her eyes that he admired; yet, it frightened him too. He had no doubt that this remarkable lady would give a good account of herself in any encounter.

"You asked about my daughter. How about your son with Mom away from home?" he questioned, changing the subject.

"My son, Donald, is doing fine back in upper state New York. He'll be four years old this month. He's with his grandparents near Lake George. I miss him a lot and will be glad when this war is over. Thinking of him makes each day a little easier to get through. Memories of happier days sustain me," she answered in a wavering voice.

He understood that it must be hard for her. He never had to deal with the death of someone that close, and could never really know how deep the pain must go or how it must influence every aspect of one's life. Memories of fleeting reunions were a common part of life during wartime. He finished his coffee and was called to Headquarters over a loudspeaker on the runway.

"Well, we say good-bye again, Lea." He placed his dirty tray on the sideboard to be washed and turned to her. She had a sad look on her face. "Until we meet again old friend."

Lea answered in a low voice. "Until we meet again, Captain. You take care now."

He reached out to shake her hand and without thinking embraced her. "And you do the same, dear lady. Your husband must have loved you very much."

She looked at him with moist eyes, lifting her lips to him, and he kissed her. It was an instinctive act that he could not control. As quickly as it happened, they released each other, and Ken silently walked away.

The bomber crews were busy checking out their planes when the DC-3 took off with the WAFS and an escort of four planes, the same ones they had delivered. Ken watched the olive drab cargo plane lift into the air with mixed emotions, then shrugged his shoulders and turned to prepare "Sweet Lori" for another run.

The return trip took them even deeper into Germany for the bombing of a tank assembly plant. They had P-38s as escorts from Africa, but they were handed off to a squadron of Thunderbolts over Germany for the return trip back to England. When they arrived over the target, it was heavily overcast which had contributed to the light resistance they encountered. Not a plane was lost. It was the most successful bomb run Ken's squadron had made so far. "Sweet Lori" had been hit by machine gun bullets near the belly turret, and Ken ordered Corporal Ranta out of the turret for the remainder of the mission.

The best part of returning home was to check the mail. Ken had two letters from Lorraine, one with pictures of Lori. At the bottom of one of the photos, there was a scrawled note of Lori's writing with the guidance of her mom. "I love you Daddy." He opened the other letter and read:

My Darling Ken,

Tonight the news on the radio is sounding a little more encouraging. A General Eisenhower has taken command of our forces in North Africa, and slowly we are taking back islands lost in the Pacific. We just had word that one of my cousins, you must remember Dave Fellows, has been wounded in the North Atlantic. We don't have any idea where he is or how serious his wounds are, but we are hopeful for the best.

I hope my prayers and love maintain a shield of protection for you my darling. There isn't a minute of the day that goes by that you are not in my thoughts. Little Lori is growing rapidly. You won't recognize her when you come home again.

I've been having trouble finding suitable tires for the Studebaker and was lucky that your father had some retreads in his barn loft that fit. Everything here is going fine. I've been assigned additional teaching duties at school. It's easier to handle two classes at the same time than I thought. The kids have been super. Most have loved ones in the service and we follow the course of the war on the Pacific and European fronts in our geography classes.

You'll be pleased to learn that I had a nice visit from one of the head foresters at Great Northern Paper Company, Mr. Herman Randall, who told me that they will have an opening for you on their staff when the war is over. Maybe that means that we should move closer to Greenville or Millinocket. I'm so anxious to have you home.

Tonight the stars are bright and I hope they are watching over you while I write this letter. Please take care of yourself, my love, and hurry back to the safety of our open arms. I love you so very much and need you more than ever.

Love and Kisses,

Lorraine

Chapter Eight

When Ken returned to the squadron from his furlough, he was better prepared to handle the emotional trauma of flying continuous bombing runs over enemy territory. He thought that with more planes and crews the stress and anxiety on the veteran crews would lessen. How wrong he was! The change increased the tempo. Bomber Command was under increased pressure to weaken or destroy the German war-making machinery. Consequently, more raids were scheduled even in difficult weather.

One night Ken and his co-pilot, Lieutenant Harry Drew, were at the Officers' Club having a nightcap after a long, hard mission. It was the only way to unwind, and alcohol abuse became a problem with those who lacked the discipline to control it. Ken had always been able to take it or leave it, but lately he was finding that it helped him to relax. Harry had a tendency to overdo it, and Ken frequently had to carry him back to quarters and drop him in his bunk. He found it amazing that after an evening of heavy drinking, Harry was alert the next day and handled his responsibility with efficiency and good sense.

This evening there were rumors running through the Club that a group of WAFS had been jumped by German fighters near the Algerian coastline while making a delivery of P-38's. Ken was disturbed by the news and contacted Bomber Command to see if there was any validity to the scuttlebutt. The officer on the other end of the line told him that it was true and that one of the female pilots had peeled off from the formation to attack the German Messerschmitt 109's. She had shot down one of the German fighters and damaged several others. Her actions allowed the formation of nineteen planes to evade the attackers and land at their designated base without incident.

Ken had a strange feeling that it was Lea and was almost afraid to ask for her name. The female pilot was shot down. Her plane crashed into the sea and was assumed dead. The staff officer confirmed that it was a Lieutenant Lea Charles, the sister of Captain Donovan Poole serving with Eighth Air Force. The news made Ken ill, and he left the smoky atmosphere of the Officers' Club for some fresh air.

He was finding it hard to rationalize that the vibrant and competent Lea was gone. He cursed the higher command who allowed them to enter an active theater of operations. He knew and accepted that nurses regularly served in the war zone. They at least had an ancient code of honor among civilized nations and the Geneva Conventions working in their favor. Lea and her friends were combat participants and as such were fair game for the enemy. The concept left him outraged and weak.

The last time he saw Lea she looked drained and tired, with lines around her eyes. There was something that had passed between them; he felt it the first time they met, yet they both chose to remain silent and not act on the impulse, except for his kiss in Africa. He scanned the sky over London and heard explosions of bombs exploding. It didn't seem possible that someone so full of life and promise could be gone.

He had known her briefly, and in that short time the aura that surrounded her had touched him, even though he was married and in love with his wife. Lea had that quiet ability to inspire respect and affection for her caring ways and flying abilities, but it went deeper than that. There was more to her than could be discovered in a lifetime. Probing the depths of her psyche could have been a glorious adventure to the one whom she admitted into her inner self. Now all that was lost, and no one would ever know… a tragic loss.

It was a clear night, and Ken instinctively searched for the North Star, remembering what she had said about it in an off-handed way. The heavens revolve around the North Star. It stands directly above the north pole and is the only star in the galaxy that doesn't move. It had been a guiding beacon to the young pilot.

That night, Ken mourned Lea's loss and felt guilty about the feelings. The war had claimed so many good people that it was impossible to mourn them other than in a collective manor. Deaths such as Lea and the young Lew Whalen were so needless. Yet his mourning for them gave significance to their lives and was his way of honoring their memories. Sleep was slow to come that night.

The next morning, he checked the weather outside the hut. It was clear and cool, a sure sign that the day's mission was a "go". He dressed, shaved and gulped down a light breakfast before heading toward the operations center for the morning briefing. He took a seat beside Harry who, true to form, looked none the worse for a night of excessive drinking. They acknowledged each other and turned to watch Brigadier General Slocum climb the stairs to the makeshift platform with the large map of Europe on the back wall.

"Good morning to you all," he began. "We have something real special for today's objective. Normally we've been assigned to strategically important locations that pertain to the enemy's war-making ability. Today we've been requested by the French underground to bomb an important staging area for several armored divisions. The SS divisions are concentrated in a relatively small area. This way we can eliminate the finished product of the factories we've been bombing. This mission is of a more tactical nature than strategic, but those who select our targets have given us the job, and it's not for us to question why."

It sounded like a change of pace, and Ken relaxed a little, relieved that it did not require a long-range penetration of German airspace. Fighter planes were assigned to accompany them to and from the target area. The crews prepared for this target with a little more enthusiasm. The fighter escorts were also to be equipped with napalm and rockets for ground targets of opportunity. Several Thunderbolts would act as pathfinders for the mission by flying twenty minutes ahead of the squadron.

The plan was to fly at altitudes lower than 10,000 feet. Intelligence estimated that anti-aircraft fire would be at a minimum because the enemy was making every effort to conceal the concentration. Ken left the briefing room with an uneasiness he could not define. Maybe it was the confidence of the higher command. He knew from experience that they could be wrong, and had the gun crews load up with even more ammunition than usual, just in case.

Soon after takeoff, "Sweet Lori" began to misfire on two starboard engines. Harry cursed the Studebaker Company who made the Wright Cyclone radial engines for the Flying Fortress, as he began to play with manifold pressure and fuel mixture controls. Soon the engines began their normal sounding hum, and everyone breathed easier.

Ken looked over at Harry. "I think you're being too hard on Studebaker. My family has had them for years. Lorraine and I have a little Studebaker Champion, and it's a sweetheart of an automobile. You aren't biased against the independents are you?"

Harry kept his eye on the instruments and gently adjusted the controls at his left between him and Ken. "Maybe you're right, Ken. My family has always had Chevrolets on our farm in St. Albans, Vermont."

"Strange," Ken mused. "I'm from Maine, so we're practically neighbors."

The mention of homemade Harry more talkative. Home represented happier days and pleasant memories. "I plan to take over the farm when the war is over. My Dad was wounded in the last war. My uncles own farms and large acreages of woodland nearby and run a Studebaker truck for logging and pulpwood. I like to work in the woods more than I do in the field."

"I'm a forester and hope to get a job with the forest products industry somewhere in Maine. If the war continues for a long time, I'll probably forget everything I was taught," Ken chuckled, adjusting the throttles back slightly while they were forming the box. Harry Drew was a good pilot and had steady nerves when the going got tough.

Their fighter escorts picked them up over the Channel. This time it was Thunderbolts instead of Mustangs. It didn't matter to the crews. Either plane was capable of handling the Messerschmitt 109 or the Focke-Wulf 190. Their target area was approximately one hundred miles inland from the Channel. They flew close to the southern French border and then set a new course to the northwest. It took a few minutes for the crews to tighten up the formation when they were hit with large numbers of German Focke-Wulf 190s. It was almost as if they expected the squadron.

Ken shortened the distance between him and the next plane in front and beside them. Every gun in the airplane was firing at the swarm of fighters. They came in attacking the formation from the side and passed below, a favorite tactic which gave the enemy the advantage, only the tail and belly gunners could fire upon them. If the Germans passed over the plane it was a sure bet that they would not survive because they became vulnerable to the massive firepower of the entire formation.

The plane took several hits from the powerful 20mm cannons in the German fighters, and as soon as it had passed, Ken ordered a damage report over the intercom. Most replied negative with only superficial damage to the fuselage.

The Thunderbolts laced into the German fighters with a vengeance. The bomber crews never had reason to complain about the courage and aggressiveness of their little friends. They did everything humanly possible to place themselves between the enemy and the precious bombers. The Thunderbolt was nicknamed the "Jug" and was famous for its ability to absorb punishment. It was a deadly antagonist in competent hands, as the enemy had discovered and gave them a wide berth.

Holding to their formation was the only option available for the bombers to survive such a punishing attack. They normally flew 1,000 feet apart at 18,000 feet. Sweet Lori sustained another burst of cannon fire which wounded one of the waist gunners and the bombardier. Three bombers had been shot down and many had been damaged, some severely. It looked like it was going to be a slugfest all the way to the target. Ken wondered if the squadron was going to survive the mission.

Something had gone wrong with intelligence! Ken no more than visited that thought than they ran into the heaviest amount of antiaircraft gunfire he had experienced. The sky ahead of them was black with flak. They had flown into a trap... The pathfinder aircraft quickly radioed back to abort the operation.

The squadron commander ordered their crews to climb to 30,000 feet and drop their bomb load. By now it was every man for himself, even if they did maintain formation integrity. They broke out of the proposed track to and from the target to get away from AA fire. That helped some but the fighters smelled blood, and they defied all precautions to destroy the squadron. Ken knew that his ventilated plane could not survive in the cold atmosphere of the higher altitude, and he broke from the formation to seek a lower elevation so that the fighters could not get below him. That equalized their chances some.

Ken was beginning his maneuver when a black object slammed into the windshield, shattering the glass. It stunned him and Harry, who involuntarily ducked their heads against the splintered safety glass chards. Two planes above them were falling apart. One had lost the port wing and was spiraling toward the ground. The sky was full of debris. Suddenly a hysterical cry came over the intercom.

"A man's body has just become lodged under my machine gun barrels," the top turret gunner screamed. "What will I do?"

Ken was occupied turning the plane to exit the area and told Harry, "Go check what's going on."

Harry turned in his seat and got the shock of his life. A man's body was stuck under the two gun barrels of the top turret. The only thing holding him there was the down pressure exerted by the gunner on the machine guns. The airman appeared to be unconscious. Harry instantly drew his .45 caliber pistol and began to shoot holes in a circle around the Plexiglas turret to create an opening to extract the airman. Harry ran out of ammunition and quickly bent over Ken to take the weapon out of his shoulder holster.

"Close your eyes, Corporal," Harry hollered to be heard over the screeching of the wind whistling through the shattered turret. Then he completed the ring around the turret and pounded his fist against the hanging pieces to make the opening large enough to haul the man through.

"Now, Corporal. Continue to keep pressure against the man's body with the barrels, and slowly step down as far as you can and still hold the guns tight. Okay you other guys, hang on to my legs and push me through the turret until I can get my arms around the man, then pull us down as quickly as possible." The task required a strong set of arms and a lot of guts, but Lieutenant Drew was up to the task.

The wind velocity was severe, and Harry hoped that the two men holding his legs were strong enough to keep him from being blown away, for only his legs were inside of the turret. The airman was still unconscious. Harry clamped the man around the back with his right arm and carefully inserted his left arm between the turret and his chest. When he was able to clasp his hands together, he ordered the gunner to pull the guns up releasing their hold on the airman. The maneuver frightened Harry because he felt as if he and the airman were being forced into the slipstream of the aircraft.

"Pull me in, for Chris sakes pull me in," he screamed at the top of his lungs. The two sturdy airmen did as he asked and slowly lowered him. "Stop a minute until I get his head and shoulders into the turret. He's coming in head first. Okay, pull us in now."

The men held the unconscious airman and carried him into the radioman's cubicle where they began to loosen the flight suit around his neck. The force of the wind outside had stripped off his boots, socks and headgear.

"Keep the man warm, wrap him up in anything in the plane to ward off shock," screamed Harry, before stepping back to the cockpit to assist Ken with the plane. He met Ken's inquiring glance and shook his head. The man's condition was unknown.

Suddenly a call came over the intercom. "He's alive, good God he's alive..." A nervous cheer erupted from the battered Flying Fortress. They had beat the odds, and one of their own was yanked from the jaws of a horrible death.

Ken knew that their race to base could mean the difference between life and death for the injured man, so he pulled the bomber down to slightly above the tree tops and headed directly for the English coast and Anglia. The white cliffs of Dover soon were visible on the horizon. Ken radioed to one of their fighter escorts for them to call ahead and have ambulances waiting for them there. Badly wounded were on board. The spectacular image of the chalk cliffs cultivated a sigh of relief from the airmen. They were almost home. The popular song "White Cliffs of Dover" as sung by Vera Lynn was the favorite song of the Eighth Air Force members.

As soon as they landed, attendants took the three wounded men away on stretchers and whisked them to the hospital. It was a weary crew that exited the plane and turned to the east to watch the rest of the squadron return. They had lost twelve planes with ten men in each! The tragic cost of the mission made the men angry. Intelligence had fouled up again, and they paid the price in blood. It was a bitter group of airmen who went through debriefing routines. The majority felt that intelligence should have picked up on the charade.

Ken had started the day with an uncomfortable feeling about the raid. His premonitions had proved to be accurate. A lot of his friends and buddies had died for nothing! It was a bitter pill to swallow. That night at the Officers' Club and the Enlisted Men's Club, the men appeared as empty husks, burned out, and spiritually depleted. Some asked over and over. "When was enough, enough?" It was a question many had asked before they were sent home as human relics that had been used until they had nothing more to give. Hope is one of the universal and human virtues that is the last to die, but even that was slowly burning down to extinction.

Ken left the Club to check the plane. The ground crew had already replaced the turret and patched up most of the holes in the fuselage. The crew chief informed Ken that it would be ready for the next day's mission. He received the news with a heavy heart, hoping that some defect would exempt them for the day. Both he and his men were at the point of nearly complete burnout.

The mission assigned to them the next day was another long range trip against oil fields in eastern Germany where they were to use incendiary bombs. Two replacements, a waist gunner and a bombardier, had reported to him early that morning. After briefing, Ken reviewed the maintenance log book and tried to swing up into the plane through the opening on the floor near the cockpit, and had difficulty doing it. Normally it was done without thinking, he had done it countless times. Today, something was missing; and it gave him a foreboding premonition like the day before. The reluctance was almost strong enough that he thought of going on sick leave. Then, Harry reached down to help him with a knowing smile on his lips, "You're not the only one to entertain such thoughts, Skipper."

Chapter Nine

The squadron assembled over the Channel and headed east toward the oil producing region of Europe. On this mission every crewman knew that AA fire and German interceptors would be particularly tenacious in protecting their oilfields – the vital blood of the war enterprise. And true to their predictions, heavy flak accompanied the squadron the minute they entered into German airspace. A large piece of shrapnel ripped a gaping hole in one of the bomb bay doors of "Sweet Lori". A few more feet forward and the plane and crew would have been blown to bits and scattered all over the German countryside.

Mustang fighters still maintained their tactically superior position slightly above and to the rear of the squadron. Enemy planes had not appeared. It was rare for the German fighters to attack when the bomber formation was undergoing heavy ground fire.

The Squadron Commander ordered the formation to climb to 18,000 feet to reduce the chances of the ground flak making a deadly hit. A second after the order, "Sweet Lori" was the recipient of a long burst of bullets and shrapnel that shattered the undercarriage of the plane. Ken instantly called over the intercom for a damage estimate.

An urgent call came from Corporal Ranta in the belly turret; "I cannot move my turret... I felt the shrapnel hitting against the turret ring... It's jammed and I can't move it to open the trap door!"

Ken felt a sick tightening of his stomach muscles. "Pilot to crew, check to see if there is anything we can do in flight to free the turret."

85

It was a frightening few minutes before the anticipated answer came over the line. "Crew chief to pilot. We cannot loosen the turret. The damage is beyond our reach underneath the fuselage. We tried to pry the turret around to the open position but were unsuccessful."

The confirmation was what Ken had dreaded. This trip was going to live up to the cautions his inner "voice" had been warning him about. They were only halfway to the target, and his heart was pounding like a threshing machine at full throttle. Events beyond his ability to alter were a normal routine in any bombing mission. He knew that, and had always accepted it as part of the war that he had signed on to fight. It went with the job. All that was left was to pray that a benevolent God would guide his actions so that his crew remained safe.

Ken was not by nature overly religious, even though as a small child he had regularly attended church with his family. As he grew older, he drifted away from regular church attendance even though he believed in the power of prayer, which had guided him through thirty-five missions over the enemy heartland, the most frightening experience of his adult life. There were few atheists on the battlefield.

As soon as they leveled off at 18,000 feet, the intensity of the flak decreased' and the German fighters took over. The sky was full of them. They boldly held off at the flanks and pumped 20 mm cannon fire into the formation at a distance beyond the 50 caliber machine guns on the bombers. Near the French-German border an antiaircraft barrage hit "Sweet Lori" several times, rocking the heavy aircraft out of formation. Ken and Harry scrambled to keep it from veering into their neighbors in formation. Shrapnel hit number three engine, and pieces of the propeller flew in every direction, vibrating the plane until Harry feathered the prop and shut off its fuel.

Some of the steel projectiles from the barrage had pierced the fuselage and hit Lieutenant Tom Castle, their very popular radio navigator. The top gunner checked on Castle and reported his findings in a stiff, controlled voice.

"Lieutenant Castle has a large cut across the neck and is bleeding profusely. He's conscious but cannot speak."

The transmission sickened Ken as he remembered the tall raw-boned Swede with a beautiful tenor voice. One of the men attending him on the floor of the bomber wrapped his neck in a large compression bandage. Tom Castle tried in vain to speak. The bandage quickly turned crimson. Terror filled his eyes as he tried to speak without success. A few minutes later he quietly closed his eyes and passed away to a place where he would never experience pain or terror again.

Corporal Ranta frantically called, "I have blood dripping into my turret."

"Lieutenant Castle has just died," a frightened voice announced.

Ken heard the messages and looked away from his co-pilot, Harry, to hide the tears that welled in his eyes and the fear that momentarily filled him with hopelessness. He began to weep and was not sure if it was out of a sense of loss from Tom's death or if it was for himself. The old premonitions of death and destruction seeped out of his consciousness and enveloped him. There was a strong desire to turn back and abort the mission. Few would blame him after being damaged so badly, but his dedication to the mission overruled his instincts, and he maintained his position in the formation.

"We're now entering German territory, so everyone be even more alert for enemy fighter planes," Ken soberly announced to the crew. "Don't be discouraged by our bad luck. We can safely fly without an engine to our target and return to base."

Corporal Ranta sat, imprisoned in his turret, and nervously replied in an ominous tone, "How can I not be discouraged and scared, Captain?"

"I understand your reaction, Corporal Ranta," Ken acknowledged his concern. "Let me reassure you that we are not going to let you become another casualty when we return. I've already worked out a solution to that problem, so bear with me, young man. If there is a God in Heaven, then he has to hear our prayers and be with us on this trip. Trust me and do not be discouraged. I've landed without wheels once, and I promise, it will not happen again."

Everyone on the crippled aircraft heard their Captain's words and searched their brains for some answers. A few passed it off as bravado to pacify Corporal Ranta. Yet, the young belly turret gunner had faith in Ken's promise and tried to concentrate on searching the skies around for enemy fighters. Harry looked over at Ken and shook his head as if to say it was impossible. Ken simply nodded his head in the affirmative and scanned the instrument panel.

The balance of the mission went off routinely, compared to the previous day. About fifty miles inside France they were attacked by German fighters. The escorting Mustangs and P-38's countered the German tactic of remaining outside of the range of bomber machine guns, by occupying the most dangerous zone of attack, thus denying the enemy their main advantage. During this last attack, "Sweet Lori" lost number one engine to cannon fire from an attacking Focke-Wulf 190. That left the plane with only two functioning engines, and they began to lag behind the formation. Three escorting Mustangs instantly attached themselves to their flanks and above the injured plane.

"Pilot to crew," Ken ordered in a stern voice. "Listen carefully. First of all, I want you to make sure your vests are in good condition. Put your parachute over the vest and secure it. Also, check each other's chute. Then, I want you to throw overboard every piece of loose supplies and equipment, including all of the ammunition, machine guns and any excess clothing on board. Hurry up while we're over the Channel because after that, I want you to put a parachute on Lieutenant Castle's body and throw it overboard so that our escorting Mustangs can vector a rescue vessel to the area. Then I'm ordering every one of you to jump."

The crisp words shocked the crew. They feverishly began to toss overboard everything they could move with their hands. Harry turned to look at Ken, knowing how difficult it would be to handle the plane alone in its current condition. He was about to argue with Ken.

"No, Harry. I've thought this out for a long time, and I'm depending on you to get the men out and into the water as soon as possible." Ken quickly grasped Harry's offered hand and steadied the aircraft. "I know that you must be wondering what's going on, Corporal Ranta. I don't have time to explain, but bear with me, friend." Ken then signaled the Mustang escorts his instructions and requested rescue vessels. They waggled their wings in acknowledgement of the request.

Ten minutes later, the plane was noticeably lighter. Even the precious Norden bombsight was thrown into the English Channel's dark blue waters. Corporal Ranta and Ken were alone in the plane. Ken was relieved that he was free to execute the maneuver he had been planning for months ever since the horrible death of Lew Whaling. His only worry now was if the two Cyclone engines had enough power to execute his plan. Ken had selected an area on the south side of the Isle of Wright where there was a sandy beach. It was too cold now for bathers so he would have the location to himself.

"This is it, Ranta. Do you read me, Corporal?"

"Yes, Sir. What are you going to do, Sir?"

"That's what I want to talk to you about. We're going to land on a beach. I'm going to flip the plane over if I can, and land on our roof. Now when I start the maneuver, I'll have my hands full and won't be able to talk. So, I want you to work hard at shaking the turret loose during the landing. The fuselage will take a beating and if you can, try to turn the barrels to the rear so that your trap door is accessible. If that works, get out of the plane and run like hell away from it. Do you understand?"

"I hear you, Captain, but what about you? Are you trying to commit suicide using me as an excuse?"

"No, Corporal. I've been tossing this contingency plan around in my head long before I knew you. Sure, it's risky, but there's a chance we can both make it, and I'm ready to take that chance. If it doesn't pan out for me, I want you to promise to contact my wife and daughter and explain what took place."

The powerfully charged conversation brought tears to Corporal Ranta's eyes. "I promise to do my best, Sir."

"Good man, Corporal. I'll call in our escorts to inform them of our plan so that they can vector recovery crews to our landing site. Get ready for a rough ride and pray like hell, son."

Sweat poured from Ken's brow down his nose. He quickly wiped his eyes to clear his vision. "Sweet Lori to escort Mustangs. Do you read me?"

"Loud and clear, Captain, I'm on your port side."

Ken checked and acknowledged the wave of the pilot's hand. "Thanks for staying with us. We've got a problem on board and am requesting you to call in all hands to assist us when we touch down."

"You have only to ask, and it'll be done, Captain," the answer came in a strong voice.

"I'm going to ditch the plane on one of the southern beaches on the Isle of Wright. My belly gunner is trapped, and I'm going to turn this baby on its head and drop it in shallow water off the beach."

"My God, Captain. Do you have enough power to make the maneuver with only two engines?"

"I don't know. If I can't do it I'm at least going in on my port wing and will have to take my chances from there. All I can do now is do my best."

"Ground rescue will be there to assist you, Captain. Good luck."

The Isle or Wright loomed in the distance. Ken leveled off at about three thousand feet, running the engines back slightly above a stall speed. Their only chance of surviving the crash depended on the two Studebaker-built Wright Cyclone radial engines to perform without incident and to give him enough power to roll into a bottoms up crash landing. As he drew closer to the beaches he noticed that the tide was out, which gave him a much wider field to execute his move. He dropped down closer to observe the landing area and made a one hundred and eighty degree turn, climbing slightly with his port wing almost touching the water. He had practiced the maneuver several times over the past few months, so it was a natural one for him to execute.

The moment of truth had arrived. To his surprise, he was calm and confident of his ability to pull it off. Images of Lorraine and Lori flashed across his mind, fleetingly aware that this may be the last conscious minutes of his life. He had developed, during his experience in bomber command, a nonchalant "what-the-hell" attitude that served him well over the past horrific months.

Aligning the heavy aircraft parallel to the water mark, Ken rolled the bomber upside down. At this point he knew that he had to operate the controls opposite from that of normal flight, and he guided the wounded plane at stall speed until the tail touched the water first and started to drag in the sand. He then killed both engines and released his seat belt, dropping him to the ceiling below.

There was nothing he could do now except to protect himself from sand and water entering the crushed windshield area. He intended to hold himself as close to the floor as possible behind the elevated platform on which the pilot and co-pilot seats were attached. He could hear the plane breaking up and desperately clung to the back of his seat for protection. The last thing he remembered was the roar of water surging through the fuselage and the salty taste of beach sand.

When the plane turned upside down, Corporal Ranta occupied himself doing what his Captain had ordered him to do – try to turn the turret to the rear. It was a strange feeling for him to be laying on his backside looking up at the sky through his turret while the gyrating aircraft was breaking up around him. He felt the tail touch down first and suddenly, the turret began to turn of its own accord. He quickly maneuvered the gun barrels to the rear and tried to open the exit hatch. Even though the plane was throwing him all about the turret, he was able to open the door and partially climbed through so as to not be pinned inside again.

Water and sand flowed through the fuselage. Corporal Ranta's first thought after he opened the door on the floor of the fuselage below him, was the safety of his Captain. As soon as the mangled aircraft came to a halt, he checked on the shore to see if rescue teams were on the scene. He breathed a sigh of relief when he saw two crash trucks and an ambulance bouncing over the sandy beach toward them. Tears of joy filled his eyes. Captain Morgan had kept his promise!

Dropping into the sandy water below, Corporal Ranta made his way through the radio room toward the cockpit area. The fuselage was two thirds filled with sand and water. As soon as he crawled through the bomb bay area a voice cried out through the waist gunner opening, "Is anyone conscious?"

"Yes!" Corporal answered as loud as he could. "I'm trying to get to the cockpit area which is filled with sand and water. Can you get a winch line on the tail and drag it inland so that the fuselage will drain?"

"We can do that," came a firm reply. "Give us a minute and we'll have you out of here."

The response of the crash truck crews was immediate. The plane began to creak and snap under the pressure being placed on it by the truck that was pulling it sideways to a dry place on the beach. Water instantly began to drain through every opening in the shattered bomber.

Corporal Ranta continued his efforts to locate his Captain, calling out to him. There was no answer. The silence frightened him. He started to dig in the wet sand beneath the pilot's seat with his bare hands. He touched something soft and dropped to his knees, furiously digging at the sand. Knowing that time was crucial, he was able to locate one of Captain Morgan's arms and pulled with all his strength. Slowly the inert body became visible until his head was out of the soupy sand. He cradled his head while the plane was being moved.

Three medics appeared at his side. "How many men are in the plane?"

"Just us two," Corporal Ranta answered in a shaky voice.

"Are you all right?" the medic asked.

Corporal Ranta shook his head and smiled, "Thankful to be alive if that's what you mean."

"Come, let's get these men out of here," a firm voice ordered.

Corporal Ranta and Ken were maneuvered to the nearest opening where strong hands pulled them from the battered aircraft. The medics deftly removed the sand from Ken's face and mouth and began artificial respiration. Corporal Ranta watched the scene. The next two minutes were the most agonizing and longest that he had ever experienced. He felt weak and collapsed into the arms of a medic who placed him on a stretcher and carried him to an ambulance. His last glimpse at the soiled figure lying on the stretcher brought a thankful prayer to his lips. Ken was coughing and turned over to vomit.

Chapter Ten

Looking back on the incident after twenty years, Ken could still feel the excitement he had created within the squadron by intentionally crash-landing upside down. Some had called it an unconscious death-wish induced by the strain of thirty-five bombing missions. Even now he was not sure what had motivated him. It was a number of things, but in reality it was simple battle fatigue; yet, if he was to be placed in that same situation today, he believed that he would make the same choice again.

He had survived the ordeal and saved the life of a fine young man who had gone on to college after the war to become a mechanical engineer at Ford Motor Company. Over the years, he and Herman Ranta had kept in touch and visited each other every few years. Ken had remained in the hospital for two days of observation. He was lucky, no broken bones and no ill effects of imbibing a certain amount of beach sand, but he was emotionally spent and had told his squadron commander that he had made his last bombing run behind the controls of a Flying Fortress. It simply was not in him to continue the grueling routine. He honestly admitted that if he was ordered back, it was only a question of time before he snapped and ended up killing himself and his crew.

The squadron commander had sent Ken home for an extended leave in the hopes that Ken would change his mind. Experienced pilots were scarce, and Ken was one of their best. Memories from the trip home remained locked in his brain. He had called the apartment from the Portland train station to let Lorraine know that he had a furlough and a gas coupon book so that he could fill the car up with gasoline. The joy that had buoyed his anticipation of being with the ones he loved was splintered by the sober tone of his mother on the end of the telephone.

"I'm coming home, Mom. Is Lorraine there? I've got extra coupons for gas if she can drive to Portland to pick me up."

"Oh, Ken, it's so good to hear your voice," his mother had openly cried into the receiver. "Lorraine isn't here right now, Ken. Your father and I came over to the apartment to take care of Lori."

"Is anything wrong, Mom? You sound kind of vague. Where's Lorraine?" he demanded.

"She had a doctor appointment, Ken. Your father can come to get you. He's ready to leave now."

"You haven't answered my question, Mom," he replied, getting more worried by the second about what he was not being told.

"She's been sick, Ken, and that's all I can tell you over the phone. Your father wants to know if you'll be at the station," his mother stated firmly.

He knew it would be useless to press the issue any further. "Tell him I'll be at the coffee counter. And be sure to tell him that I have coupons for gasoline and will fill the car up when he gets here."

"He's on his way, Son," his mother exclaimed with a sigh.

It was a long wait. Ken filled the hour with ugly images thinking that maybe Lorraine had had an accident of some kind or that she had some rare disease his mother was too frightened to tell him about.

Ken anxiously met his father, Ken Sr., outside the coffee shop with open arms. His father had aged since the war had begun. Deep lines radiating from his expressive eyes and his mouth were more pronounced. His brown hair had turned gray and become thinner. Ken, Sr. was a bulwark of traditionalism in an era of rapid change, and the aura of confidence that seemed to surround him was still there. Ken loved the values that defined his father and could never recall of an instance when he lost control of himself. He came up to Ken's chin. The two men embraced in a strong bear hug. In this unsettled time when war casualties were mounting, it was a moment each were thankful for.

As soon as they were on their way to Gray, Ken questioned his father. "Dad, can you tell me what Mom could not about Lorraine? I've just about gone out of my mind imagining all kinds of things. How sick is she anyway?" It was more a demand than a request.

Ken, Sr. was prepared for the inquiry. "Son, there's no way of being gentle about Lorraine's condition. She's a very sick girl and it pains me to have to tell you. To sugar coat it would only postpone the inevitable.'

Even more alarmed by the statement, Ken shouted, "My God, Dad. What's wrong?"

"Lorraine has myelogenious leukemia and has had it ever since the two of you married. For most of her life it was not a factor that concerned her. Then, after Lori was born, she began to notice symptoms of fatigue and lack of stamina. Large black and blue spots would appear on her body wherever she banged herself, even a light bruise would develop and last a long time. She blamed it on the heavy work load at the school with fewer teachers available and being on her feet for long stretches of time. She went to see a doctor who checked her blood count and gave her the news. The excessive numbers of white blood cells originating in the bone marrow were the cause of her lethargic condition and lack of appetite. She's lost a lot of weight, Son."

The news was so unexpected that Ken could not immediately grasp the situation. He recalled that she had seemed strained and tired the last time he was home. He had thought nothing about it, and she never mentioned anything wrong. He had attributed it to the fact that he had just burned their cabin down.

"Did she know about the disease the last time I was home?"

"I don't want to speak for Lorraine, but I believe she knew by then. Her white blood cells, the leucytes, have been abnormal for almost two years," his father recalled, reaching across the seat to his son's hand. "Don't be angry, Son. She wanted to shield you from the worry. She's a brave girl, and we love her as if she was our very own."

"Are you telling me, Dad, that this disease is terminal? If so, how long does she have?" he asked in a loud voice.

"You've got to be strong. I can't answer that, but Lorraine will be honest with you."

The ride back home was a long journey. He had just come from the battlefield where death and destruction were the norm, where he and every other veteran had become hardened to that stark reality. But that was war, and this was his home, where death or the thought of death shattered his soul. It just can't be happening to Lorraine who did not deserve such an unjust burden in the prime of her life. Dedicated teachers like Lorraine should be exempt from such a calamity. He was having trouble rationalizing the facts, and more than ever, he felt guilty of how badly he had treated her.

Mixed emotions ran through his mind. At first he was proud of her silent courage, and angry that Lorraine did not let him share the burden of her disease. He was her husband and had the right to know, to share, and possibly comfort her. The second they turned into the driveway, Ken jumped out from the car and ran into the apartment. His mother, a matronly dark-haired lady with bright eyes, met him at the door and fell into his arms, speechless. Tears of joy and sadness mingled as they rolled down her cheeks.

He felt like a little boy again and clung to his mother. In that moment of reality they both began to cry, slowly at first, then with increased convulsive sobs of fear and angst of the road ahead of them. Ken released all of the sadness he had been containing on the ride home. How he had yearned for the soft comfort of his Lorraine. Now, he questioned if he had the courage to support and care for her the way she had always done for him.

* * *

Now, twenty years later, Ken could still feel the pain of that tragic homecoming.

* * *

97

Little Lori was two years old and had been frightened by all of the sadness that accompanied her daddy's sudden visit home. Standing by his mother, she was lost and confused with the display of so much grief. She had two small braids with red ribbons tied on each end. Ken had leaned over to take her in his arms.

"My darling Lori has grown since I last saw her," Ken had said, holding his daughter. In that moment of need, he knew that he had to reach down into his inner reserve to find the strength to do what had to be done. It was his turn to shoulder some of the responsibility.

Lorraine succumbed to the ravages of high fever brought on by her inability to fight off diseases that ended her young life. She had been hardly able to sit upright in bed to greet Ken when he rushed to the hospital to see her. The image of her lying on the white sheets looking much like a small child after losing so much weight was still vivid in his memory. The moment he laid eyes on her, the first thought that entered his head was that she "was dying before his eyes." A weak smile had crossed her cracked lips and the first words she uttered was an apology for the way she must look to him. Pale, fragile, and close to death's door, Ken was completely distraught when he was faced with the reality of her frail condition. It required all of his power to control the emotions that overwhelmed him. She was too weak to carry on a meaningful conversation. The fever was running amok in spite of the massive amounts of penicillin being used to counteract it.

She had pressed an envelope in his hand with a request that he not read it until she was gone. He had nodded in agreement with tears filling his eyes. She saw his reaction and began to cry turning her head on the white pillow so that he could not see her. The pillow was stained with her tears. He squeezed her hand and felt her weak response. He had witnessed valor and courage on a daily basis in the war, but seeing his Lorraine fight the ravages of the disease she was afflicted with was beyond any comparison. How wrong he had been to accuse her of being unfaithful. Guilt feelings for his unfair outbursts and the insane act of burning their log cabin, the one place where she might have been able to find some peace and comfort in the final months of her life. He hated himself for being so judgmental and selfish. He had only thought of himself.

Somehow Ken found the strength to take control of the situation and insisted that he care for Lori while his parents returned to their home to rest. The days ahead would require all of their energy and fortitude, and it was only prudent that they do as he wished. He took it upon himself to contact Lorraine's sister Aline and her mother, Mrs. Carr. His mother-in-law was in a nursing home suffering from hardening of the arteries to the point where she did not recognize anybody. She was probably unable to understand the gravity of her daughter's illness, but Ken felt it his duty to have the caretakers inform her anyway.

He was preparing himself for the dreaded day ahead of them, and when it finally arrived, he found how inadequate his measures had been. The doctor had called him at 3:00 AM, two days after his arrival. Ken heard the words and, in a trance, asked the doctor to repeat the message. The kindly physician cleared his throat and slowly began, "I have the sad duty to inform you that your wife Lorraine has just passed away. She had lost the battle to fight the disease that took her life. I can tell you because I was with her to the end. Her passing was peaceful and pain free. The staff and I want you to know how bravely your wife fought this terminal disease. From the very beginning, she knew what was going to take place; yet, she never gave up fighting. She earned our respect and affection even though all we could do to help her was to make her final journey without discomfort."

Thanking the doctor and hospital staff for their kindness and compassion, Ken hung up the phone. Little Lori was standing in the kitchen doorway staring at her daddy. She had been awake when the phone had rung. He kneeled down and pressed her to his heart. She knew that something terrible had taken place. The look on her Daddy's face frightened her. For a long time they clung to each other. He continued to hold her close as he told her, in a trembling voice, that her mother had just gone to Heaven.

"Mommy told me she would have to leave us, and she would always be watching over us," Lori whispered in his ear.

It was still dark when Ken bundled Lori in a blanket and stepped outside the apartment. He oriented himself and searched the northern skies until he saw the north star.

"That star, the biggest and brightest one, right up there at the top of that branch, Lori," Ken pointed to the top of a large sugar maple tree. "They call it the North Star. Your Mommy always liked to locate it at night. I would not be surprised if she found her place in Heaven near that star."

"Can we go there to see her?" Lori innocently asked.

"No, Honey, I'm afraid the distance is too far for humans like us," he answered, staring into the darkness. "Your Mother is now one of God's angels. She was called home to be your guardian angel, my dearest little girl."

Just then a soft breeze brushed their faces as if to confirm what Ken had said to his daughter. It was a powerfully spiritual moment when Ken could "feel" Lorraine's presence. As quickly as it began, the breeze died down, and they were left alone in the dark to cope with their sorrow. The immediate future looked grim. How could they cope with their sorrow and face a new day without the guiding touch of their beloved wife and mother?

The day of Lorraine's funeral was one of the longest and most exhausting days Ken had ever had to experience. He was drained before it began, and by the time it ended, he was a physical and emotional wreck. The small town had turned out in large numbers. Lorraine was a very popular teacher to students and parents alike. He stood in line as friends and neighbors passed by to pay their last respects and shook his hand. He was ready to run away and scream for everyone to leave him alone so that he could mourn the death of his wife.

Each night after Lorraine's death, Ken sat alone in the kitchen and read and re-read the note she had prepared for him. He could recite it by heart:

To My Darling Husband,

I am writing this letter to you from my hospital bed, and it is important for me to let you know how much it pains me to give you the sad news of my illness. The doctors have assured me that my time is near and that I should be prepared to face the inevitable and prepare you and the family.

I can tell you truthfully that for the past year, since I was diagnosed as having leukemia, my life has been filled with sorrow that I will not be with you to care for you as you so graciously deserve, my love. You have been my life and my reason for living. I want you to know that I will be as close to the two of you as death allows, always. Look for me on a clear night when the north star is shining bright. I will be with you even if you cannot see me. I'll be there. Think of me when the sun sets at the close of a lovely day and when the soft breeze rustles the colorful leaves of fall. Think of me when the loons call in the darkness of night and when the sweet aroma of spruce and fir fill the air. We always shared and found strength in the tranquility and solitude of the forest. Please, my husband, try to find that source of strength once again. I'll be with you always and forever.

Our daughter is such a precious little girl, and I'm saddened that she will grow into womanhood without me. Remind her how much I love her and that I will share her life from afar. My love for her and for you, my dear husband, is absolute and forever. It is my wish that you may find someone to share your life and to be at your side for it is not normal to be alone. If you can be blessed with another love, please do not carry any guilt, for you and whomever you may choose will have my blessings.

Always know that I love you with all of my heart and I will be waiting for that day when our Lord calls you home. Until then, dear love, good-bye...

Lorraine

Chapter Eleven

After the funeral, Ken had applied for and received an extended furlough in order to settle family affairs. Once the hectic pace of the funeral and burial services were completed, he felt a severe physical and emotional fatigue. He desperately needed solitude so that he could sort out the immediate future. Long range plans were unthinkable. He was even having trouble thinking ahead for the next meal he and Lori were to eat. On that note, he decided to leave Gray and drive to Savage Pond near Moosehead Lake where he and Lorraine had occasionally gone to "get away" from things.

Savage Pond was accessible by a "fair weather" gravel road established by the Great Northern Paper Company. It was unimproved in the winter and definitely not accessible during the spring mud season. There was a small rustic cabin on a peninsula where the pond could be seen from three sides. The cabin was built by his father and uncles during the depression years as a place for hunting and fishing. They paid the Great Northern a dollar a year for a ninety-nine year lease. The cabin held fond memories over the years he and his father had used it for hunting and fishing trips. It was a little too "rough" for his mother to enjoy extended stays, so she usually stayed at home, but the men in her life had fond memories of the camping experience.

Not much in the way of improvements had been done to the cabin. It had a single hole outhouse in the corner of a woodshed attached to the east side of the cabin. There was no running water, but a stream that ran into the pond was right beside the cabin. The water was always cool and pure to drink. On the west side of the cabin a small cellar was dug and lined with rocks as a place to store excess foodstuffs in tight metal containers so that moisture and rodents did not contaminate them. Excess matches, kerosene, and canned goods were placed in the cellar for safe keeping. A heavy cedar trap door covered the cellar.

When Ken was a small boy, a trip to the camp entailed a hike of three miles. The only thing that had changed was the construction of an improved road so that it was possible to drive right to the door in an automobile. He had liked the cabin better when it was more isolated. It had given him a greater sense of accomplishment by just walking in over the rugged terrain. He and Lorraine had spent their honeymoon at the cabin, so it held wonderful memories of happier times for Ken. They had a strong attraction to the log cabin and decided to duplicate it on the piece of land they owned in Gray.

Ken had talked to his mother and father the night after the funeral about taking the trip with Lori. The apartment had no appeal to him and, he was anxious to move their stuff out, but he had no idea where he was going.

"What am I going to do about Lori when I leave?" he had asked them, seeking some direction.

"For now, Son. Why don't you leave Lori with your mother and I until the war is over. She's comfortable here with us and is no bother," his father told him. "If we need a helping hand, Lorraine's sister Aline is most willing to help whenever possible. After the war you can make up your mind about what you want to do. Beyond that I wouldn't even attempt to make any specific plans."

"Will you settle things for the apartment?" Ken asked, feeling guilty that he was burdening them with his responsibilities.

"Of course we can. It doesn't make sense to pay rent any longer than necessary. The owner of the building is an old friend," Ken's mother replied, running her hands through his short hair. "I think a trip up to Savage Pond will do you and Lori some good. The roadway has been upgraded and you'll find another cabin has been built a quarter mile beyond ours. A rich business man from New York purchased a large parcel of land from Great Northern and built a gorgeous two story log cabin on the water's edge."

Thoughts of a retreat to Savage Pond was an immediate goal that made him feel better. It was a start, and he made preparations for the excursion. The next morning he and Lori loaded the Studebaker coupe with warm clothing and supplies and headed north, purchasing groceries at Greenville on their way.

As soon as he left Greenville behind, the magnitude of the Maine wilderness brought all of his senses alive. It was a sunny day with a cool nip in the air that gave promise of the severe winter months ahead. The smell of spruce and fir swept across the landscape, filling his lungs with the cleansing scent. The land always invigorated and enriched his soul. He was doing the right thing. Here in the wilderness, a haven of solitude, he was hopeful that he could plot a future course for the life he and Lori would pursue together.

Just as soon as he turned onto the road to Savage Pond from Kokadjo, warm memories that had faded away sprang back to life. Once again he was a small boy fishing off the small dock he and his father had built years ago. The water was deep enough off the end of the dock that he could not touch bottom when he jumped off. His father suggested that he pick up a heavy rock and jump off with it in his arms. It took him to the bottom where he dropped it. By then Ken had run out of air and panicked until he broke out of the dark silent water. From that day on he was more comfortable and confident with himself in the water, but he never took another trip to the bottom with a rock!

He had brought along Lori's small training potty chair so she would be perfectly comfortable in the cabin without having to worry about using the outhouse. She had fallen asleep on the seat for a short ways. After they stopped at Greenville for provisions and refueling of the coupe, she stood on the seat with her left arm around her daddy's shoulder. Feeling her tiny fingers around his neck thrilled him. She was a precious child. Up until a few days ago he had been a total stranger to her. Now they had become buddies and Ken drew strength from the fact that she was his responsibility, and he looked forward to his role as her parent. Actually, he readily admitted, she needed him less than he needed her. On top of all the sorrow that filled his heart, his love for her had been a source of renewal and hope. He silently prayed for guidance to be worthy of the memory of his Lorraine.

Lori had again asked if they could go to see her mother, and he did his best to explain that even though her spirit always filled their hearts, she was in Heaven, a different place where humans cannot go. He doubted if she was able to grasp what he was trying to tell her, but it seemed to satisfy her curiosity.

The day after they arrived at the camp, they had completed cutting some firewood and were enjoying a meal of baked beans and hot dogs, a staple food in the Maine woods, when they decided to take a walk along the shore to their new neighbor's cabin, anticipating that the owners were probably back in New York. Ken promised Lori that if the walk was too much for her, he would give her a ride on his shoulders.

She asked him for a lift about a hundred yards into the trip, so he hoisted her to his shoulders. She grasped him tightly around the head. He held onto her two legs dangling over his shoulders. She seemed so small and light, a perfect miniature little girl. His love for her was increasing by the hour. She clasped her hand over his eyes, and he made believe he was bumping into a tree. She laughed, and he laughed with her. How precious that little laugh had been. She made him feel important, and that transformed him and gave him a reason to embrace the future. This trip into the wilderness was working its magic.

They spotted the building in the distance. It was a luxurious cabin with brick chimneys. He was surprised to note a curl of smoke coming from one of the chimneys. Someone was home. Then, Ken saw a float plane tied up to a long dock that jutted into the water. It looked like a two-seated Aeronca. He was familiar with them and knew that they had a small Continental engine.

Wondering if he and Lori should leave instead of intruding on their neighbor's privacy, they were spotted by a German shepherd dog who approached them barking loudly. "It's okay, Honey," Ken calmly explained to Lori. "The dog is simply curious about us."

The dog continued to bark, standing off at a distance from them. Ken called in a calm, deliberate voice and held out his hand to the dog. The shepherd began to wag his tail. Ken knew then that the dog's barking was just a bluff.

A man stepped out from a second story balcony on the front of the house and called to Ken, "Hello."

"Hello," Ken waved to him. "We're camped out at the cabin south of you and stopped by to introduce ourselves."

"Yes, well, we'll be right down. The dog is harmless. His name is Rex."

Ken called to the dog. "Come here, Rex." The shepherd carefully approached him and nuzzled his outstretched hand.

A few seconds later a couple appeared on the dock in front of the cabin. They were his age, dressed in hunting clothes. Ken had forgotten that it was deer season. He stepped up on the deck, keeping Lori on his shoulders.

"I'm Kenneth Morgan, and this is my daughter, Lori. We're your neighbors."

The stranger was a tall, handsome man with dark hair and complexion. Ken figured that he was probably Italian. There was an indifferent air about him that discouraged familiarity. "I'm Lauren Mackenzie, and this is my wife, Jean. We flew in for a few days of hunting."

"We're pleased to meet our neighbor," Jean Mackenzie said, extending her hand to Ken. She was an attractive blonde with an easy smile and a pleasant disposition in contrast to her rather stiff husband. "I see that Lori has the best seat in the house." She extended her arms to lift Lori off his shoulders. "You're a lovely little girl and we're pleased to meet you."

"Won't you have a seat," Lauren Mackenzie said, pointing to several Adirondack chairs on the deck. "I remember your father helped us build the cabin."

"Dad mentioned that to me," Ken recalled, taking a seat. Lori quickly left Mrs. Mackenzie's side and sat on his lap, a little uncertain about the strangers. "My, what a beautiful cabin you have. I never thought I'd see something like this on Savage Pond."

"It was something my father-in-law wanted to do. We use it for hunting and vacations," Lauren explained, appraising Ken, noticing the fatigue jacket and the cap. "Are you in the service?"

"Yes, I'm a bomber pilot on furlough," Ken was unwilling to volunteer any more about himself. "Lori and I are going to be up here for a few days. How do you like your Aeronca?"

"Oh that's a company plane. I've just recently learned to fly it," Lauren briefly answered.

"Well, Lori and I have got to get back," Ken announced, standing up. The conversation was strained, and he had no desire to prolong it. "We're glad to meet you both. Best of luck hunting."

"It was nice of you to drop by," Jean Mackenzie said. She seemed nervous and avoided making eye contact.

Ken had a feeling that the two were completely out of their natural environment. The Maine woods normally cultivated a sense of neighborliness and caring – these two people did not belong to that club. He lifted Lori onto his shoulders for the trip back to the cabin. They waved to the Mackenzie's as they stepped off the deck. Mrs. Mackenzie waved, but her husband turned and walked away. Ken decided then and there that Lauren and his flashy wife were not his kind of people. He was glad to leave. It was an awkward encounter, and he vowed that there would not be a repeat performance.

For two days Lori and her father cleaned the cabin and cut firewood for the ravenous fireplace and the small cook stove at the other end of the cabin beside the entrance door. He talked to Lori as if she was an adult. She knew a lot about him, such as the fact that he did not like to eat the heels of a loaf of bread, and absolutely refused to eat oatmeal or asparagus. He found it amazing that Lorraine had shared those simple things about him with their daughter. It made him miss her even more.

He was carrying a heavy load of guilt. He had failed to appreciate his dead wife as much as she had deserved and that fact cut him to the core of his soul. How could he have been so callous and insensitive to the one who loved him with such complete devotion? In the still of the night he often lay on the bunk bed staring at the dying embers of the fire with tears in his eyes. Images of Lorraine filled the cabin everywhere he looked. An emptiness and feelings of inadequacy and unworthiness enveloped him.

Several days later after Ken and Lori had cleaned up from a supper of fresh salmon and fried potatoes, Lori climbed into her bunk on the west wall of the cabin next to the fireplace and dozed off while her father got out a few candles to read by. It was just beginning to get dark when a loud knocking sounded at the door. Ken had just placed a few logs on the fire and answered the door. He confronted a very nervous and hysterical Mrs. Mackenzie, "What's wrong, Mrs. Mackenzie?"

"Please, may I come in?" she asked in a high pitched voice.

"Of course, take a seat next to the fireplace. Is anything wrong?" Ken asked again, guiding her to the cot in front of the fireplace.

Mrs. Mackenzie was completely soaked, her clothes dripping with water. She was on the verge of collapse. She started to shiver and her teeth chattered so that she could not speak.

"Listen, Mrs. Mackenzie, we can talk after you've had a chance to dry out and warm up." He went to his suitcase on the bunk above Lori, grabbing an armful of clothes and turned to the frightened Jean Mackenzie. "I'm going to draw the curtain around this cot so that you can get out of your wet clothes in privacy. This was the cot my mother used when she came to the cabin. Here are a pair of clean pajamas and a clean bathrobe for you to change into while we dry out your clothing. While you're doing that, I'll put on a pot of coffee or hot cocoa, take your pick."

"A hot cocoa would taste good. I'm so sorry to intrude like this," she cried in a wavering voice.

"Neighbors help neighbors in the Maine woods, Mrs. Mackenzie. I'll toss a couple of clean towels over the curtain to help you dry off. They're still in the car, we didn't finish emptying it. I'll be right back."

While he was outside he heard an airplane engine running. Shortly, he looked to the west and saw the plane lift off the water. It was dusk with total darkness only minutes away. He thought that Lauren Mackenzie had to be a complete idiot to be flying from an unlit body of water at night. His first uncomplimentary opinion of the man was reinforced by this display of reckless behavior at best.

"I just heard the plane take off," Ken announced, throwing the towels over the curtain. "Cocoa is coming right up." He checked on Lori who was sitting up in her bunk watching everything taking place. "We have company, Honey. Mrs. Mackenzie has come for a visit and needed to change her clothes because she was all wet and cold. Would you like some cocoa too?"

"Yes, Daddy. I like it anytime," she answered.

"How about if we have a jelly donut, too?"

"Okay, Daddy."

Five minutes later, Mrs. Mackenzie drew the curtains back against the wall beside the fireplace. She was dressed in the pajamas and robe and backed up to the crackling fire. She was still shivering. Ken picked up Lori and placed her in one of the chairs beside the cot. "I'll bring the cocoa over here on the small table in front of the cot. Lori is going to join us for cocoa."

Jean Mackenzie turned to look at her. Some of the tension had drained from her face. "Hello again, little girl. I didn't mean to break up your evening like this, but I was so cold and didn't have any other place to go."

"You don't have to apologize to us for your actions. I talked myself and Lori into a jelly donut; would you like to join us?"

"That sounds like fun," she replied with a hollow laugh. She placed her wet clothing around the fireplace to dry and took a seat beside Lori. "How old are you, Lori?"

"I'm three years old, and I can count to ten and say my abc's," she confided to the lady with the wet blond hair.

"Her mother was a teacher," Ken explained, pouring the cocoa.

"My mother is in Heaven," Lori innocently told her.

"Her mother just passed away this week. We came up here to search for some guidance. I've lost my way and need some help," Ken explained to her.

Mrs. Mackenzie looked first at Lori, then at Ken. "I am so sorry. Please forgive my sudden intrusion. I've imposed myself upon you at such a hurtful time. Forgive me. If I had known, I would have never bothered you," she exclaimed.

Ken served a paper plate filled with jelly donuts. "Help yourselves." He placed another log on the fire. "A fire always feels good up here regardless of the month." There were many questions he wanted to ask the visitor, but he refrained from being too inquisitive.

"Thank you for the cocoa and jelly donut," Mrs. Mackenzie said, watching the flames leap around the fresh birch log. "It's been a long time since I had cocoa. It tastes good."

"You're very welcome. Now, I don't mean to pry into your affairs, but let me say that you're welcome to stay here for the night, or if you prefer, we can take you to the nearest inn or hotel in Greenville. Before you give us your answer, let me say that I just came from Bomber Command in England where looking out for each other is not only a way of life but a privilege. You're not a burden to Lori or myself."

She heard and understood what he was trying to tell her. Tears welled in her eyes. She brushed them away with the sleeve of the bathrobe and said, "My personal problems seem so insignificant to what you and Lori are experiencing. I do apologize, my timing was terrible. You must be wondering what happened out there to me. Without going into detail, my husband and I had a terrible fight and were ready to leave the cabin. At the last minute, while the plane was warming up, I told him that I did not want to fly in such a stressful period. I begged him to turn back to the dock. He was so angry and worked up over our personal affairs. He's not the most competent pilot in the air, and had been drinking some and got angrier than I've ever seen him. He hit me beside the head. I was frightened and jumped out of the plane into the water nearer to your dock than to ours. I'm a good swimmer so I headed for the lights in your cabin. The water was bitterly cold. He swung around toward your landing and then turned back to our dock."

"Your husband showed some real bad judgment flying off a pond at night without adequate lights. There could have been a floating log in his path and he would have never seen it. He's lucky. You showed courage in exiting the plane the way you did. Now, you tell me what you want to do; remember what I just said."

She took a bite from the jelly donut and said, "I'm afraid that I had not thought about anything except to get away from him. He's real bad when he gets angry. My purse is still onboard, and the only clothes I have are now drying. I can't get into the cabin without a key."

"I can imagine that you must be worried about your husband. Why don't we wait a few more minutes for your clothes to dry, and we can drive to Kokadjo to use the phone at the store. We can check with Folsom Airways to see what the status is of your husband, and delay any decision until we know how he's doing. What do you say to that?"

"You're very kind, and I appreciate it."

Twenty minutes later, Ken bundled Lori with a Hudson Bay blanket and placed her in the storage area behind the seat of the business coupe. Ken held the door open for Mrs. Mackenzie and ran around to start the Studebaker. By the time they arrived at the small store, Lori was asleep. He grabbed his flashlight and entered the outside phone booth, leaving the heater going in the coupe to keep it warm. An agent from Folsom's acting as air coordinator for the Greenville area answered. Ken knew the man personally and asked about

Lauren Mackenzie. He was told that Mackenzie had fueled up and filed a flight plan from Greenville to Plattsburg on Lake Champlain, where he intended to stop off for the balance of the night. It was a little over a hundred miles to Plattsburg, and with good instruments it was not a difficult route to follow. Ken was relieved and thanked the dispatcher.

"I spoke to the dispatcher who said that he was on his way to Plattsburg."

"That was the route we followed to Greenville," Mrs. Mackenzie informed him. "Thank you. I feel better now."

Ken turned to look at her in the limited light of the store. "What do you wish to do, Mrs. Mackenzie? I can drop you off at Greenville where you can get a train to Montreal, and then drop down into New York or maybe you can pick up a charter flight. It's up to you. I'll gladly loan you the funds to do whatever you wish."

She remained silent for a while exploring her options. Without a warning, tears filled her eyes and she began to cry. Ken took a clean handkerchief from his pocket and handed it to her. After a long spell she was able to pull herself together and blew her nose. "I'm so sorry. I was simply wondering what Lauren was thinking by leaving me here alone. For all he knew I might have drowned..."

Chapter Twelve

Ken could appreciate the troubling thoughts that worried her. "The important thing, Mrs. Mackenzie, is that you're all right. I'm not emotionally equipped to get involved in your personal affairs. Let me just say that being neighbors, like we are, obligates us to try and do the right thing. I pledge my honor as an officer in the United States Army that you will be safe and your personal reputation respected."

Tears still filled her eyes. "I just want to lay down and rest for the night. I'm exhausted."

"Then that's what will be made available to you, Mrs. Mackenzie."

The next morning, Jean Mackenzie awoke early to find Ken and Lori already sitting at the small table eating a bowl of cereal. She suggested that she should go to her cabin to get into some different clothes she still had there, letting herself in by breaking a window in the shed.

"I could drive you over there," Ken offered.

She wrapped the bathrobe around herself and took a seat beside Lori. "No. It will do me good to walk. Good morning, Lori. My, you and your daddy got up so quiet that I did not hear a thing."

"Do you like corn flakes?" Lori asked her.

Ken had already set out a bowl and spoon for their guest. "I don't normally eat very much for breakfast, but yes, I like corn flakes."

"Please help yourself," Ken placed a pitcher of milk and the sugar bowl in front of her. "I've also got a pot of coffee on the cook stove. Would you like a cup and maybe a donut>"

114

She smiled at him. "Thank you, that would be fine. I'll have a small bowl of cereal with Lori first. I am hungry this morning."

"As soon as you're finished at your cabin, I could pick you up, and we can go to Greenville to see what time the train is running. It's a Canadian Pacific line to Montreal or to Portland. I doubt if you'd be able to locate a charter flight to New York."

"I appreciate your help," she replied with a reserved look on her face.

An hour later, they were on their way to Greenville, with Lori standing on the seat between her father and Mrs. Mackenzie with her arm around Ken. They were in luck that a train was due within an hour for Montreal where she could make connections to New York. When the steam engine rolled into the station, Lori was frightened and Ken picked her up and held her.

"What can I say for being so kind and considerate to a stranger? I promise to send you the money you've loaned me for the trip just as soon as I arrive back home," Mrs. Mackenzie confronted them.

"We wish you a bon voyage, Mrs. Mackenzie. I hope that you and your husband can successfully reconcile your differences. Lori and I are going back to Savage Pond to try our luck at fishing for some salmon."

"Goodbye, little Lori."

"Bye-bye, Mrs. Mackenzie," Lori said, waving her hand at her.

"You take good care of your daddy, Honey," she looked up at Ken and said, "I leave this place with pleasant memories of how a potential tragedy was averted by caring neighbors..."

The conductor announced a loud "all aboard."

Mrs. Mackenzie hugged Lori and gently kissed Ken on the cheek. "You take care of yourself, Captain Morgan." Then she stepped onto the train.

Ken and Lori watched the train leave the station and disappear around the bend. He placed Lori on the ground and slowly walked to the coupe. They stayed at the camp for three more days until one morning when it began to snow lightly. Ken was anxious to leave and did not want to have any difficulty getting out of the road. They quickly placed all the linens and blankets in a roll and suspended them in the center of the cabin on thin wire so that the rodents would not make nests in it. Then they left. Once they arrived at Gray, the first thing they did was take a warm bath.

That evening, after Lori was in bed, Ken sat around the kitchen table with his mother and father and told them that he was going to cut his furlough short. He had a feeling that he could work things out just as well by reporting for duty. The short retreat with Lori had given him some time to think things through for him and Lori. He had arrived at a plan which included applying to the Great Northern Paper Company for a job after the war. If that materialized, he would move into the Moosehead Lake region with Lori.

The fact that he was transferring out of Bomber Command had already been confirmed by the new orders that came while he was at camp with Lori. He was ordered to report on or before January 10, 1944 to Edwards Army Air Corp Base in Los Angeles, California, where he was enrolled in a short training course in fighter operations. The course focused on new tactics and gunnery specifically for the Pacific theater of operations. Ken had made up his mind that waiting around at home for time to pass would actually be more difficult than the training schedule that was ahead of him.

He said his good-byes, tearful though they were, and had his father drive him to the Brunswick Naval Air Station where he picked up a flight to the west coast. Three days later, he was in California trying his flying skills at the controls of the new improved P-38 Lightning attack fighter and the latest bubble canopy Mustang P-51 fighter. After trying both, he had to agree with Lieutenant Lea Charles, they were both superb aircraft, but the P-38 with its heavy firepower of machine guns and a 20mm cannon concentrated in the nose pod was as she had put it, "an artillery platform with the soul of a racer." The mustang was slightly faster but the Lightning had a much longer range. Both aircraft were fun to fly, but Ken preferred the twin fuselage P-38.

It rekindled his love of flying, and the accelerated training schedule he attended helped to displace the grief he still carried for Lorraine. Every night he retired to his tent in the sandy desert and wrote to Lori and his parents. It was those quiet moments when he was alone with his thoughts, that the same old hurt returned, sometimes resulting in another sleepless night. He still carried a heavy burden of guilt and could not get the thought out of his mind of Lorraine suffering from a terminal illness at the same time he was accusing her of unfaithfulness.

The progress of the war was the main topic of conversation among the men attending flight school. The North African campaign had finally ended, and the surrender of Italy allowed the allies to concentrate on the defeat of Germany and Japan. Ken was informed that operations in Germany were, for the moment, adequately staffed, so he would be used in the Pacific theater. The P-38 was especially adapted for the long range flights endemic with the war against Japan. The aircraft had a range of over 2200 miles, almost twice that of the Mustang. Ken had to brush up on his navigational skills. In the bombers he relied on navigators to do all of the work. In the widely spread out islands of the Pacific, navigational skills were as important as flying skill.

Finally, on April 15, 1944, Ken was ordered to the 18th Fighter Group as part of the 13th Air Force, then serving as MacArthur's private air arm under the command of Lieutenant General George Kenney. Ken had briefly served with Kenney at a flight training school in Maryland in 1941.

He touched down on an airfield in New Guinea April 15, 1944. His introduction to the tropics was the stench that permeated every pore of his body as soon as he landed. The smell of rotten and decaying vegetation hit him like a heavy blow as soon as he stepped from the DC-3 transport plane. It was a fetid scent that he never got used to. It tainted every bit of clothing, even the taste of food that they were served.

New Guinea still had sections that were occupied by the Japanese, especially along the northern coastline. Most of the fighting involved air, naval, and amphibious forces under General MacArthur's command. The operations were planned and executed with precision and had relatively lighter percentages of loss when compared to the assaults made by the marines under Admiral Nimitz. Fewer losses were a trademark for MacArthur throughout the rest of the campaign to the end of the war, even though he had to contend with the best troops and commanders in the Japanese Army and Navy.

Ken first saw his brand new Lightning the day after his arrival. It was sitting in a graded parking area being serviced by his ground crew. He introduced himself and was impressed with the dedication and skills of his field maintenance crew. The relative crudeness of the runway and temporary nature of living and service quarters was typical of the war in the Pacific. Everyone slept and worked out of tents. He had received his tropical area shots from the medics before arriving, and his arms still were tender.

He was the squadron executive officer and was given a briefing of future operations from that airfield. Primarily the Mustangs gave ground cover for assaults from the sea and advancements once the Army had established a foothold ashore. The new Lightnings carried a full load of ammunition and two 500 pound bombs as well as an optional fuel tank for extreme distances that could be dropped if necessary. The P-38 had the longest range of any attack fighter plane in the war.

His squadron's first assignment was to "soften up" the area of advancement of Army troops near Hollandia. Ken led the squadron because the commander was laid up with malaria, a disease that most everyone contracted. It was a debilitating illness with life-threatening consequences, and every man religiously took his quinine prescriptions as requested.

On this first flight, Ken met for the first time the fabled Japanese Zero fighter plane. It had been the fastest, most maneuverable, and most successful fighter of the war, up until the Mustang, Thunderbolt, and Lightning became available to

Allied forces. Nevertheless, the Zero was a formidable foe with skilled pilots at the controls. The Zeros hit the formation from above and for the first few moments of combat, Ken was impressed with its ability to turn sharp corners and to climb and dive.

Ken ordered the squadron to tighten up its formation and for the four outer aircrafts to engage the enemy. He too climbed out of his point slot to assist them. He was still fully loaded with ammunition for the cannon and machine guns. The Lightning was faster than the Zero. Soon he positioned himself slightly above and behind a Zero and lowered his nose until he held the enemy plane in his sights, then he pulled the trigger and slowly lifted the nose, effectively stitching the Zero full of holes from front to rear. He overshot the Zero and went into a steep climb observing that the plane was burning and losing altitude. It had been his first "kill" and, somehow, it did not make him feel good.

Without warning, he had to make a hard turn to starboard to avoid a mid-air collision with one of his own planes. "Sorry Ken, I was not paying attention," his wingman called over the radio.

"Neither was I," Ken replied, looking for enemy fighters. After dispatching the three Zeros that had attacked them, he ordered the squadron back to their "v" formation which allowed them greater flexibility than the box he had flown with the bombers.

While the battle for Hollandia was raging, he and four members of his squadron had participated in a long-range patrol out over the Pacific to report anything unusual and to attack targets of opportunity. They found a collection of Japanese barges loaded with supplies being pulled by a sea-going tug. Each of them strafed the vessels in a low level approach and immediately climbed and turned to the port. The barges exploded with a horrific bang the fighters felt several hundred feet away. On that same patrol, Ken was able to shoot down two more Zeros. It was not that difficult a task with the magnificent P-38. The more he flew it, the more he liked it. It was a perfect compromise of speed, power, and maneuverability. It gave him a feeling of invincibility. He especially liked the smooth, quiet operation of the Allison V/12 engines. One was capable of keeping the plane in flight, so it was a more secure craft to fly than a Thunderbolt or Mustang.

For several weeks Ken flew combat operations along the New Guinea coast. He had been faithful in taking his atabrine tablets, yet he succumbed to the crippling fevers that accompanied an attack of malaria. He was shivering so much his teeth chattered, and he could not get warm. Chills and hot flashes alternated within his body, leaving him completely bed-ridden. He was moved to a Naval Hospital ship that followed the progress of the advance toward Japan.

For days he saturated his sheets with sweat while the efficient staff fought to control his spikes of high fever. Slowly his attacks became less frequent and severe. He was then able to take more liquids which his body desperately needed. The nurses supplemented his liquid intake with intravenous glucose. The illness left him weak and exhausted, but he was able to sleep well and was slowly regaining his strength. One day a nurse stopped by his bed with some letters in her hand.

"These are for you, Captain," she said, placing the mail in his hand. "Would you like for me to crank up your bed so that you can read them?"

"That would be fine, Ensign, thank you."

The first letter he read was from his mother:

April 10, 1944

My Dearest Ken,

A few words tonight to let you know that everything is going well for us here at home. Lori has adjusted remarkably well to our household. She's an adorable child and we are fortunate to have her. She has so many of Lorraine's soft and considerate mannerisms. She asks often for her mother and questions us why Heaven can't let her mother come for a visit. It's sad, but we are handling the situation the best we can.

Your letters have been most helpful and encouraging for your father and me. He has been keeping a daily diary on the progress of the war both in Europe and Japan. I think often of what it is like for you over there in the midst of so much conflict, and I become frightened for your welfare and of all the brave young men who are fighting. It seems as if the war will go on forever. We pray for your safety, my Son. Come back to us, Ken, your daughter and family need you.

I saw Aline last night. She takes Lori frequently. I find her much more sober and sad since Lorraine's passing. Your wife was a beloved person in this town. I find it amazing how many people mention to us how kind and considerate she was. Always cheerful and willing to help, her students idolized her. I understand they are having a difficult time adapting to the new teacher from Bangor.

I took the liberty of opening the enclosed letter from a Mrs. Mackenzie. She enclosed a check of $100.00 which your father deposited in your checking account.

Take care of yourself, dearest Son. We pray for you and send our love across the miles to protect you.

Love,

Mom and Family

The letter was typical of his mother. Even if things were not going well at home, she would never tell him. He unfolded the letter from Jean Mackenzie:

Dear Neighbor,

As I promised, I'm sending a check for the money you so kindly advanced to me. Thank you so much for your understanding and considerate reception of a stranger who imposed herself upon your private world at such a sorrowful time for you. You handled it with grace and kindness and I will never forget that it was sincerely and honestly extended to me.

Give a special "hello" to Lori for me. I've thought often about her since. You are probably no longer at home and wherever you are in the horrible war that is raging across the seas, may God keep you safe and bring you home to your daughter.

Again, thanks for everything.

Jean Mackenzie,

November 25, 1943

P.S. You may be interested in knowing that my husband, Lauren, and I have separated. It was inevitable after his conduct on that fateful night. Perhaps when the war is over, neighbors can get together over a cup of cocoa and a jelly donut. I hope that may be possible.

The last sentence brought a smile to his cracked lips. The friendly note made him feel good. The next day he was strong enough to pen a reply:

August 14, 1944

Somewhere in the Pacific

Dear Neighbor,

I did not receive your letter until today. Thanks for the prompt check.

I am no longer flying bombers. When I returned to duty I went through a refresher course to fly fighters. It has already contributed to my appreciation and joy for flying.

The censors would only blank it out if I was to tell you where I am, so I'll save the space. Lori and I stayed at the hunting cabin for several more days after you left. It was a retreat that I needed to do and it gave me a chance to get to know my daughter a little more. Now that I am primarily responsible for her welfare, I hope that I'm up to the task. My parents are doing a wonderful job with her and obviously, her dad misses her very much.

I wish that I was back on Savage Pond fishing for salmon, but we have a job over here to finish and I'm proud to be a part of that effort. With God's help I'll return one day and share that cup of cocoa and a jelly donut with you and Lori.

Until that time, I wish you all the best.

Your neighbor,

Ken Morgan

P.S. Incidentally, I have just received notice of my promotion to Major and you are the first to know.

Chapter Thirteen

Major Kenneth Morgan served as Assistant Squadron Commander of the 400th Fighter Squadron from May 1944 to the end of the war with Japan. The psychological trauma of flying bombers had been greater than flying the P-38 fighter bomber in combat. However, the tour of duty he did under MacArthur's command took more out of him. Living in the stench and extreme heat and humidity of tropical jungles drained him physically. He lost twenty-two pounds and could still detect the sour smell of the rotting vegetation which made up a large part of the tropical forest in every meal he ate. How he yearned for his beloved Maine woods and the clean aroma of spruce and fir. When the war was over, he vowed to never go near another so-called tropical paradise. He had had enough.

The squadron flew almost daily in support of MacArthur's drive to liberate the Philippines as he had promised. Those officers who knew and understood amphibious warfare were impressed with MacArthur's virtuoso performance in conducting multi assaults against defended beachheads. They were consistently done with fewer losses than the operations being conducted in the Central Pacific by Marine forces under Admiral Chester Nimitz. It was a tribute to MacArthur's brilliance as a tactician. (*Note at end of chapter*) As the campaign entered the Archipelago that made up the Philippines, Ken personally flew several photographic missions, taking advantage of the speed and long range of the P-38. He flew over strategic locations in a grid fashion at speeds over 400 miles per hour. Several antiaircraft guns fired at him, but he was never touched by a single bullet.

Occasionally, he and his squadron were ordered to simply fly at low speeds and altitudes over the prisoner-of-war camps located primarily on Luzon. Those flights were a thrill and raised morale one hundred percent, seeing the skeleton-like figures waving to them from the barbed wire compounds. Ken and three of his pilots escorted two B-26 bombers over the prison compounds so that they could drop hundreds of small "Victory Packages" small packs with chocolate, cigarettes, paper and pencil and encouraging markings on the package such as "I Shall Return". Later, they all learned that the Victory Packages, a product of MacArthur's staff, were the greatest morale booster for the prisoners who had almost given up hope of survival. Ken's small contribution to the success of the flyovers gave him his greatest sense of achievement. Seeing firsthand how they had created hope out of despair made him proud to be an American.

By the time Victory in Europe, V/E Day, was announced May 8, 1945, Ken was feeling extreme fatigue. The war had several more months to go, and he wanted to be a part of that last push which made the Japanese surrender. Malaria again struck him down, and he was evacuated by air to Pearl Harbor to the Army Hospital at Schofield Barracks located in the mountains north of Pearl City. He was back on American soil! He was there a week before he became conscious enough to realize where he was. His first thoughts were for the squadron. He never believed himself to be that indispensable man, but he truly did not want to miss that last punch that brought Japan to the armistice table.

While he was recuperating in the large ward, he heard someone mention a Major Don Poole who had flown in England with Bomber Command. He was Lea Charles' brother. Ken had never met him, but his co-pilot Jim Reams had flown with him. Celebration within the hospital wards was loud and heartfelt. Those who had suffered for the cause of freedom had more right than anyone else to commemorate the cessation of combat. The hospital staff set up a table with a bowl of punch and snacks to nibble on. They also relaxed the banning of alcoholic beverages for the occasion and set a tub filled with beer and ice on the table. It was enjoyed by all.

Ken was still weak from the malaria but was improving every day. He wanted to be with his buddies today. They gave him a wheelchair and wheeled him into the largest ward on the floor. He knew none of the patients by name and asked for a Major Donovan Poole. The nurse who was pushing his chair steered him to the corner of the ward to a bed with a cage filled with wires supporting the patient's two legs done up in casts and his left arm. Ken cautiously approached the bed and saw that the patient was partially sitting up, watching some of the crazy antics of his roommates. Surprised at the full head of grey hair, Ken found him to be older than most of the pilots he knew.

Ken asked, "Are you Major Donovan Poole?"

The patient slowly turned his head as if it hurt him and looked at Ken. "I'm Don Poole," he said, slightly slurring his words.

"I'm Ken Morgan. I heard you were here, and I wanted to stop by and to say 'hi' to another veteran from Bomber Command."

Don Poole studied him for a few moments. He was a powerfully built man with wide shoulders and large hands. "Now I remember where I've heard your name. You're the pilot who landed his Flying Fort upside down on the Isle of Wright. Congratulations, I often wondered if I would have the guts to do that. I'm glad to meet you. When did you come to the Pacific?"

Ken had told him why he transferred to fighters, including the loss of his wife Lorraine. He then asked Don why he had left The Eighth Air Force.

Don took a drink of water through a straw and answered, "I was selected along with several other fliers with a lot of flying experience at the controls of two and four-engine planes. We went to the west coast to participate in a special operation program involving sudden erratic maneuvers in the B-29 Super Fortress. That plane is a monster, and the one we

126

flew on practice flights had a lot of mechanical failures due mostly to quality control, or the lack of."

"Are they easier to control than a B-17?"

"Not really, Ken. They're so big that there's a delayed response to controls, but it's amazing how sturdy they are. I was selected because I flew a two-engine DC-3 for years before the war, hauling the U.S. Mail. A week ago I went through a set of handling procedures which included an emergency landing at two hundred and fifty miles per hour."

"Wow!" Ken exclaimed. "That's almost suicidal."

"That's why I'm tied up in this rigging," Don smiled. "The minute I touched down, a landing strut failed, and I was pulled off the runway into a forested portion of the field here in Hawaii. I demolished the plane, but I survived. I never knew what the project was all about. It was very hush-hush. Obviously, I'm no longer a member of the crew that was selected."

"I'm sorry to hear of your bad luck, Don. I knew that you served in Bomber Command because my co-pilot Jim Reams told me he had flown with you. He was one of our best, and I lost him on one of our missions."

"I remember Jim," Don replied in a reflective mood. "We've lost a lot of good people. I only hope that the people back home are worthy of the price being paid for our freedom. Early in the war I lost one of the finest men I've ever known, a young West Point Captain who died at Bataan. I miss him still..."

Ken had held his tongue. He wanted to ask about Lea and decided that this was neither the time or place to bring up subjects filled with heartache. A few minutes later, Ken said so-long to Don and promised to visit again soon. A nurse wheeled him back to his bed. He was exhausted and was not in the mood for festivities.

The next two weeks were filled with ambitious physical therapy exercises to tone up his body. At first he walked a short distance to the point of complete exhaustion. A few days later he continued the walk and extended his distance every day until he was capable of walking several miles without extreme fatigue. He frequently stopped by Don Poole's bed to visit and pass the time of day. They became good friends with one thing in common – their love of flying made them kindred spirits. Not once had Don mentioned his sister Lea, and Ken respected his privacy by never bringing up the subject, even though he was bursting to question him for further details of her demise.

Ken was impressed with the positive attitude Don exhibited in regards to his injuries. The doctors had assured him that he would come out of this tragedy with the use of all of his limbs after a long painful period of physical therapy. He readily accepted the challenge and began to plan his future. He told Ken that he planned to create an air charter company serving the northeastern United States and Quebec, Canada, specializing in float plane insertions of hunters and fishermen at isolated locations. In that respect, he was using the famous Alaskan bush pilots as an example.

The conversations they had on the subject whetted Ken's appetite for the endeavor. Sometimes the two talked well into the early morning hours about the proposed project. It was good therapy for both of them, and the nursing staff encouraged the exchange of ideas with coffee and snacks. Don drilled Ken about the potential in the northern Maine wilderness for such an enterprise, and Ken mentioned that the Great Northern Paper Company would probably be enthusiastic about the idea because it would provide an increased amount of fire protection to the forest fire patrol flights they had installed prior to the war.

By the first of June, Ken was ordered back to his squadron, flying out of a recently bulldozed airfield on Leyte. His primary mission was to fly close ground support for the advances taking place in Luzon. The island was secured by December 1, 1944, and efforts turned south to the largest island in the Philippines, Mindanao, where he flew missions in support of the assault by the Eighth Army under General Eichelberger.

He was located at a new airfield on Mindanao when they received word that on August 8th, 1945, an atomic bomb had

128

been dropped on Hiroshima. Ken had wondered about the B-29's that had carried out the mission and surmised that Don Poole was probably selected as a backup pilot for the operation.

Three days later, news of a second atomic bomb dropped on Nagasaki stunned the world. The soldiers and sailors desperately hoped that it spelled the end of the war. Their dreams came true six days later when the empire of Japan unconditionally surrendered. It was a glorious day for those who had survived the ugly crucible of war. A collective sigh of relief and thanksgiving passed around the world. Now was the time to bind their wounds and get on with their lives.

* * *

Ken had remembered that fateful period with great clarity. It was one of the milestones in his life, and he never forgot how it had been. The joy that there would be no more death and destruction was tempered by sorrow for those who were not going home, and there were many – almost 300,000 military men and women were killed in combat in the most destructive war in history.

An uncontrollable feeling of sadness accompanied his elation over the surrender. He too had indulged in the reverie associated with the welcome news, but he also correctly realized that the moment would soon fade into history, mourned only by those who had lived and survived the nightmare experience. The sudden ending of the fighting stimulated an unquenchable thirst to return home to their families to pick up on their lives where they had left them, following a long tradition in American history.

They had left hearth and home as young men fueled with rage to avenge the madness Japan and Germany had perpetrated upon the civilized world. The men that returned, many with broken bodies and minds, entered a world that had changed, and many found it difficult to assimilate back into society. The war had robbed them of four years of their youth. Time stood still for nobody.

A voiced called from the ground. "Colonel, Colonel Morgan, are you all right, Sir?"

Ken awoke from his trip down memory lane and recognized Herman Ranta calling to him from the ground. He could still remember the very young belly turret gunner who had experienced their famous or notorious crash landing.

"Yes, I'm okay, Herm. Standing here on this platform like this, it was easy to recall how it had once been. I didn't realize I'd been here so long." Ken consciously turned from Herman and wiped the moisture from his eyes.

Herman saw the gesture and understood. "I just wanted to make sure that you'd have enough time to get back for events scheduled tonight at the banquet room."

Ken reluctantly retraced his steps, joining Herman on the ground. They walked towards the waiting taxicab. The air was saturated with memories and the spirits of thousands of young men who never came home. At the end of the runway near the roadway, the two veterans paused and turned for one last look. Neither saw the tufts of weeds or broken pavement, or the rusty Quonset hut partially standing, succumbing to the ravages of time. Instead, they saw and heard the mighty roar of Flying Fortresses struggling to get airborne for one more mission. They could even feel the thunder of hundreds of powerful engines screaming for liftoff. The noise obliterated every other sound for miles. The scene was a permanent part of their memory, and when they were gone, no one would ever know just what had taken place...

* * *

(*) It is worth noting that the Marines conducted less than twenty landings during the war; whereas, the Army, under MacArthur's command, conducted over eighty landings against far greater concentrations of Japanese troops, and they captured twenty times more enemy territory. Yet, the literature glorifying the Marine Corps grossly exceeds that which covers the major land battles in the Pacific under Army command. It reflects a distorted view of historical fact.

130

Chapter Fourteen

Ken and Herman were reflective and silent in the taxicab. Herman Ranta reached into his coat pocket, pulling out a pamphlet, offering it to Ken. "I just read a paragraph about the bombing missions written by Ernie Pyle during the war. He probably felt the same horror that all of us shared."

Ken took the booklet and read:

"It was just that on some nights, the air became sick and there was an unspoken contagion of spiritual dread, and we were little boys again lost in the dark."

Ken passed the pamphlet back to Herman. "I knew that he had flown several missions with us, but I never met him. 'Lost in the dark,' how appropriate those words are."

Herman had noticed a definite reticence in Ken's demeanor that had not been with them on the flight from Boston to London. "Are you happy that you came, Colonel?"

Ken appreciated what the youngest member of his bomber crew was trying to say. "Sure, I'm glad I came, Herman, and I'm especially pleased to make the trip with you and your family. It's hard to explain, but the minute we boarded the plane and left Boston, my thoughts have been dominated by events of the past, some of which triggered the same old feelings that I thought had died long ago. This trip has unleashed memories that are as vivid now as they were then, and I'm a little overwhelmed. It's not that I'm unhappy about coming to the twentieth reunion, to the contrary, it has enveloped me to the degree that it's almost as if I was transported back in time."

"You don't need to explain to me, Sir," Herman told him. "I think you just described what is happening to all of us. How could we have experienced what we did and not be influenced by its severity for the rest of our lives? It's only normal."

Ken silently shook his head in agreement as the taxicab stopped at the inn to let them out. Herman was excited and turned to Ken, "The banquet hall will be packed tonight. I'm going to take a shower and maybe a short rest for the evening's events."

"That sounds like a good idea, Herman," Ken said. "Actually, I'm more tired than I expected, and tonight will be an occasion that I would not miss for anything. Seeing old faces will be a welcome experience. I'm glad you goaded me into coming."

"It would not be a proper reunion without you, Colonel. I'll see you later at the banquet hall."

"I'll be there," Ken replied, walking towards his room. He, too, showered and shaved again for the very special evening ahead. Taking Herman's suggestion literally, he stretched out on the bed and rested. The minute he closed his eyes he was mentally transported back to the years and events that had preceded the trip.

* * *

When Victory in Europe Day was celebrated, there was spontaneous rejoicing, but when Victory in Japan Day arrived, pandemonium broke out all over the civilized world like one loud thunderclap echoing across the land. He had been stationed at a field in Mindanao. When the Japanese signed the surrender document on the deck of the USS Missouri, Ken had already received orders to return to Fort Devens. Those who had served the longest in the theater were the first to be discharged.

By that time he had made up his mind not to pursue a career in the Army. His daughter Lori needed him, and he needed her. However, he did join the Maine National Guard so that he did not have to resign his commission as a major. Later, in 1948, he was transferred from the United States Army

Air Corps to the United States Air Force, a separate military organization equal to the Navy and Army. Airpower had come of age.

The first day of his arrival home by train was, by choice, a quiet reunion with his parents and Lori. The only thing he really wanted to do was to spend some time getting reacquainted with his daughter.

His father informed him that a contractor in town had offered $5,000.00 for the land the cabin sat on. The announcement started him thinking about something he had wanted to do for a long time – improve and upgrade the old hunting cabin on Savage Pond so that it could be used as a year-round home. The $5,000.00 would give him a chance to build his dream house, so he accepted the offer. It would give him and Lori an opportunity to build a whole new life.

The morning after his arrival home, Ken was up before Lori so that he could visit Lorraine's grave by himself. It had been difficult returning after a prolonged absence and not having her there to welcome him home. It rekindled his sense of loss. The headstone was in place, and he noticed fresh flowers in a vase at the base of the stone marker. He read her name, date of birth and date of death as if he was reading about a stranger. Removing his hat, he kneeled beside her grave:

"I made it through the war, Lorraine, as you already know. Many times I thought I'd never survive. I still love you and treasure the memories we shared. I'm not sure how I'll do without you, but I'll do my best; please guide my footsteps. I'm at a crossroads in my life, and I'm afraid that I'll make the wrong choices. I do not have as much time to carry out the work God has for me to do, because of the time spent in the war. Maybe that was all part of it; I'm not able to judge. All during the war, all I could think about was doing my duty and caring for the men in my crew. They were my responsibility. Now that has been removed from my shoulders, and somehow it has made me feel vulnerable and insignificant. I want to make up for lost time, but I don't know how. Guide me, my love, and when you are near, as I know you are now, give me some sign that I can be sure."

He uttered the last sentence, and a soft breeze passed across his face like a caress. Suddenly, tears formed in his eyes and dropped off his chin onto her grave. He remained kneeling for a long time, quelling the longing in his heart. He had come to the grave not simply to pay tribute to his deceased wife; he came searching for forgiveness for his punishing treatment of her at a time when he should have been comforting her and helping to carry the heavy burden she accepted with courage and grace. He returned to the house, saddened by her absence but strengthened by the fact that he had been able to outline a plan for the future.

It was mid-September when he and Lori relocated to the old cabin on Savage Pond to commence their construction venture. She was as enthusiastic as her dad about the project. They christened the cabin "Shangri-la" after the earthly paradise so beautifully described in *Lost Horizon*, the popular novel by James Hilton, a book he had read three times during the war.

Three Years Later – Summer of 1948

Ken and Lori were putting the finishing touches to the completed cabin. Lori had recently finished her second grade at Greenville Elementary School and was off for the summer months. The diesel-powered generator had been functioning for a year, and a gas hot water heater and cooking stove were installed, which functioned without electricity. The first project had been to build a suitable septic system and to dig a well for water.

The cabin bore little resemblance to the original structure even though they did retain the fireplace wall and portions of the left and right hand walls which acted as interior walls for two bedrooms on either side. The new cabin was built toward the pond from the old cabin, twice as wide with a second story including two bedrooms and large balcony with a magnificent view on all three sides. Downstairs were two bedrooms, a study and a large great room which included the living room, kitchen, bathroom, and utility room. Ken was adamant about building a deck across the front beneath the balcony with a set of stairs leading to the balcony. The cabin was homey and relaxing. He wanted it to reflect his modest tastes and did not want it to become a showplace like the Mackenzie's had built. He didn't have the financial resources to build one anyway. He wanted to live in it, not occupy it.

Their first visitor of the summer was Jean Mackenzie who drove in the driveway in a brand new 1948 Mercury convertible. Ever since the end of the war she had been a frequent visitor to the cabin belonging to her father, and she always stopped by to spend some time with Lori and Ken. The summer of 1947 she showed up for a few days during her vacation with a new boyfriend, Tom Murray, a good-looking young veteran officer from the Marine Corps that Ken didn't rate very high. The first time they met there was an unspoken antagonism between the two men. He was too much concerned about his elevated position in life and looked upon others as inferior. Ken had a difficult time treating him with civility for Jean's sake.

The last time the two saw each other was when Jean was leaving Savage Pond for the season, and she stopped to say good-bye. Ken generally wore his Army fatigue clothes while working on the cabin. Tom looked about to see what was taking place and assumed, "You must have been one of those doggie ground pounders in the war."

It was a derogatory remark that belittled the Army infantryman. It hit Ken like a slap in the face, resenting the arrogance and insensitivity of the man. "No, I had the privilege of flying close air support for those doggies as you put it, and I have always been proud of the valor and courage they displayed to the world every time they met the enemy. For your information, I resent your term doggie."

"I can't believe you said that, Tom," Jean quickly rebuked him and continued. "Major Morgan is a highly decorated pilot, and I, also, take offense to your remark."

Tom Murray turned beet red. "I apologize for my choice of words."

"I accept your apology, Tom Murray," Ken answered with a firm set to his jaw. "I know that you marines did a great job in the Pacific, and I would never question their courage and sacrifice; however, do not be misled by the voluminous amount of literature coming from the Marine Corps into believing that you won the war in the Pacific. The fact is, the Marine Corps made fifteen opposed amphibious landings. Contrast that to the eighty-seven opposed landings made by MacArthur's forces from New Guinea to the Philippines, and you can draw your own conclusions as to the degree of effort applied in the Pacific."

The delivery of facts from Ken caught Tom off-guard, and he mumbled to Jean that it was getting late and they had to get along.

A year later, Lori was the first to see Jean getting out of the car and ran to greet her. "Hello, Mrs. Mackenzie!" she cried, enthusiastically leaping into Jean's open arms. "I just got promoted to third grade next year."

"That's wonderful, Lori," she replied, picking her up. "My, you've grown since I saw you last fall. Pretty soon you'll be a young lady. Where's your Daddy?"

"He's up in the woods with our new truck, cutting firewood. I hear him coming now. We've finished the cabin, and I've got a surprise inside."

"What would that be?"

"Come, I'll show you," Lori said, leading her by the hand into the cabin through the French doors leading into the front of the great room.

Jean looked about to see how they had completed the cabin and moved furniture in place. "My, you and your Dad have done wonders to the room. It has a warm, comfortable feel that fits him. What did you want to show me?"

Lori asked her to close her eyes and then turn around. "Okay, you can open them."

Jean slowly turned around and opened her eyes. There in front of her was a beautiful upright piano tucked snugly into the corner of the wall. "Oh, it's beautiful, Lori. Can you play anything on it? I can't play a note."

"I'm taking lessons from a lady in town once or twice a week. My Daddy told me that this piano belonged to my mother. It was my Christmas present this year." She sat down at the piano and lifted the cover. Her small fingers picked out the scale two times, and then she slowly picked the notes of TWINKLE TWINKLE LITTLE STAR.

Ken had watched quietly listening to his daughter play. He clapped when she was finished. "Well done, Honey. It's nice to see you again, neighbor. How've you been?"

Jean recognized his voice and ran to embrace him, kissing him on the cheek. "Hi, neighbor. You two have been busy since last fall. It's beautiful, Ken. I had to break away from the rat race for awhile and come up here to find myself again. I envy you being here year-round."

"Say, I like your new Mercury. Come let me show you our new truck," he said, leading her to the doorway and pointing to a brand new green Willys Overland pickup truck backed up to the woodshed. "It's got a six-cylinder engine with four-wheel drive like the Jeeps. So far, we really like it. It rides harder than my Stude coupe, but we'll get used to it."

"It's an ideal vehicle for you two, especially in the winter time. By the way, would you have any such thing as a jelly donut and a cup of cocoa?" She laughed at the request. Ever since her untimely invasion of their privacy, it had become a tradition that had cemented their friendship.

"We just got some fresh ones this morning," Lori replied.

"I'll turn on the water. We can eat out on the new picnic table on the deck and christen it properly with our neighbor and the tastiest treat this household can create," he laughed. Lori smiled with him. She liked it when her Daddy was happy like that. The first year after the war, he didn't laugh at all. She served the donuts in their original carton and set a plate, napkin and spoon for the three of them.

Ken poured the cocoa, placing a dollop of marshmallow fluff in each of the three cups, and sat down opposite Jean. "Are you and that marine still a couple?"

Jean blushed at the mention of Tom Murray. "No, that was a mistake I won't make again. I apologize to you for his inappropriate behavior. We fought all the way back to Albany. You really touched a nerve with him when you mentioned the contrast between MacArthur's contributions in the Pacific theater. All he could do was disclaim your facts. Later, I checked on the situation, and you're correct. He was a bore. His father and mine are good friends. I've known him for several years, but we were hardly what you called a 'couple,' Ken."

He always thought it strange. Jean was a very attractive young woman from a wealthy family that could afford anything she wanted, yet he had always found her to be well grounded in everyday values that he grew up with. She never forced herself upon others or assumed that she was entitled to special treatment as a result of her heritage. As a matter of fact, she was shy and very reserved. He enjoyed her company because she was sincere and honest and very much a straight talker. She was comfortable and confident with who and what she was.

She had married Lauren Mackenzie, a cheap alcoholic opportunist that had abused her and cheated her out of thousands of dollars before she finally divorced him. Tom Murray was probably a rebound relationship.

"I can tell you now," Ken looked at her sitting comfortably on the deck with the breeze softly blowing her loose hair. "My opinion of Murray was not positive when you first introduced him. He had too much mouth and too little backbone."

"My father made similar remarks about him," she replied, anxious to change the subject. "How do you like your job at Great Northern?"

"I find the work challenging. I've had to bone up on some basic silviculture and management practices, but that goes with any profession. I like it better now that we've finished with the cabin. Incidentally, I have a surprise for you two," he said smugly, looking at his wrist watch. "Within the next couple of hours, you'll know what it is."

"That's all you're going to tell us?" Jean asked with an inquisitive look.

"Yep, that's all I'm going to say for now." He smiled at Jean and then looked at Lori, who knew what he was talking about. He placed a finger over his lips as a signal for her to not divulge the secret.

"Is this related to the GNP job?" Jean asked.

"In a way, yes," he briefly replied.

"You're teasing me, Kenneth Morgan."

"I'm really sorry that I brought up the subject. I should have contained my enthusiasm, but that's all I can say right now. Do you want a hand opening up the house?"

"I was hoping I could coax you into turning on the gas heater and starting the diesel generator engine. I was also wondering if we could install some sort of short wave radio at the log cabin," she said, finishing her cocoa.

"I should tell you that the Central Maine Power Company is planning to install a power line up our road within the next year or so when supplies of material are available. They predict that more customers will connect to the line if it's already there. With that in mind, I wouldn't even bother with a shortwave, Jean."

"I like that bit of information. That'll give us electricity and a phone line, which I'll find handy in case of emergencies. Well, what do you say if we go over to my cabin in the Mercury? Here are the keys; you can drive it."

Ken drove the new convertible to the cabin and stopped under the carport. "This is a fine automobile. The V/8 engine is whisper quiet, and you can tell it's got a lot of power. It's a good choice, Jean."

"I didn't pick it out; my father did."

"You know, Jean, you and I have been neighbors and friends for a couple of years, and I've never heard you talk about the kind of work you do, or the line of business your father is in. If I'm asking too many questions, just tell me to mind my own business."

"It's no great secret. I assumed that you knew that my father is in the construction business, and I work for him as an architect. I design buildings."

Ken smiled knowingly. "Now a lot of things fall in place, especially your knowledge of home building. If I'd known that, I'd have picked your brain more about a lot of things."

"You had some definite ideas you wanted to pursue and your efficient layout is great, Ken. There are no magic rights or wrongs in design; it's all a matter of taste. Your craftsmanship is superb, and the cabin reflects your preferences for simplicity and functionality. I like that," she confessed, getting out of the convertible.

"Say, I didn't expect to get psychoanalyzed on the basis of my carpentry," he joked. He was learning more and more about this lady whom at first glance could be characterized as a typical socialite, but that would be wrong. There was more to her than that. He was finding her to be good company and her ability to be herself made other people around her feel comfortable.

Ken immediately went to the utility room after Jean opened up all of the doors and threw open some windows to air the house. He turned on the gas heater and threw the master switch on the electric fuse board, then went outside to start the diesel engine. A few weeks before the company who delivered the diesel fuel had installed new batteries. The Detroit diesel engine started after a couple of turns, belching black smoke from the stack. After warming up for a minute the exhaust cleared, and the engine ran free. The load placed by the engagement of the generator temporarily pulled it down a few revolutions and then settled into a steady hum. He liked the sound of an engine running well. He had installed the same size and brand of diesel generator as Jean's family.

While they were busy at the house, Ken heard the sound of a plane from the southwest and shortly a Grumman Goose two-engine amphibious plane flew low over the water and began a turn to land. He waved to the pilot and called for Lori and Jean.

"Here comes my surprise. The pilot is a friend of mine from the war. Great Northern authorized me to purchase a surplus plane from the Coast Guard. I'll be responsible for its maintenance and am the designated pilot for the company. Its home base will be here at Savage Pond."

Chapter Fifteen

The pilot landed the aircraft in the middle of the pond sending up a plume of spray, and headed for the dock which protruded forty feet into the pond. Ken told them that the plane was capable of landing either on water or land, which made it a useful plane for the North Country. The pilot opened the door, throwing Ken a line to secure the craft to the dock.

"Welcome to Maine, Don," Ken embraced the tall, muscular pilot dressed in a one-piece flight suit.

"It's good to be here, Ken. The plane is a beautiful flyer, steady and predictable. You'll notice it's a little more sluggish compared to your P-38 though. I can understand why the Coast Guard liked this model for their search and rescue. It's agile and sturdy. It sits kind of low in the water which may take a little getting used to, but that drag brings it to a stop quicker than a set of brakes."

"Don, I'd like to introduce you to my neighbor, Jean Mackenzie, and my daughter, Lori."

Donovan Poole was a strong man with gentle mannerisms. "Hello, Mrs. Mackenzie, I'm pleased to meet you."

Jean offered her hand. "It's nice to meet a friend of Ken's."

"I'm especially happy to meet the lovely little girl 'Sweet Lori' in person." Don towered above her, so he kneeled down to give her a hug. "*Sweet Lori* will live forever as a legend in the history of the Eighth Air Force. Your daddy pulled a stunt that still stands as a miracle. Maybe you're that miracle."

Ken was alive with excitement admiring the airplane. "Do you have time for a maiden flight with me at the controls?"

142

"That's why I delivered it, Ken. You can take it up and drop me off at Folsom's in Greenville where I've made arrangements to fly back home," Don answered, checking his watch.

"Sounds great!" Ken exclaimed enthusiastically.

"Okay, let's crank it up," Don replied. "There are four seats in the rear. So you ladies can be back seat drivers if you want to go for a ride."

"That would be fun," said Jean. "I've flown quite a bit; what about you, Lori?"

Ken looked down at his daughter to check if she was ready to take her first plane ride. "You know, Honey, if you don't feel right about it, you and I can do it some other time. It's up to you. Daddy would never ask you to go if there was any danger."

"Are you going to drive the plane?" she asked apprehensively.

"Yes, I am, and I'll be very careful with you and Jean on board."

Jean placed an arm around her shoulder, "If you prefer to stay here, I'll stay with you, Lori."

"I'm a little scared, but it might be fun," Lori gave her father a hollow grin.

"Me too, Honey," Jean agreed, accepting a helping hand getting on board. She strapped Lori in one of the four seats and took one next to her.

Ken studied the instrument panel and controls for several minutes. Don pushed the plane away from the dock and pointed out the levers for the wheels to convert the flying boat into a land aircraft. Finally, confident that he had familiarized himself with the aircraft, he turned to Lori and Jean.

"I'm ready to start the engines now, so don't be frightened if they're noisy. After that, I'm going to turn the plane around and take off. The ride will be rough for a while until we become airborne. Are you ready, Lori?"

"I'm ready, Daddy," she replied.

The steady hum of the engines sounded good to Ken's trained ears. All the time he flew bombers and fighters in the

Army, he never stopped listening for any sign of malfunction in the engines of the plane he was flying. He started his run down the pond, pushing the throttles for full power. Holding the craft in a straight line, Ken slowly pulled the stick back and broke the hull free of the water, turning slightly to port as he lifted off. Then he headed for Moosehaed Lake and made a turn close to the high cliffs at Kineo.

The plane responded easily to controls. He turned to see how Lori and Jean were doing. Lori was glued to the window the moment the ground began to drop away from the aircraft.

"This is fun, Daddy. The boats on the water look small."

Jean had been watching Ken go through a transformation from an enthusiastic little boy with a new toy to the very serious and responsible pilot she knew he was. She could imagine how difficult his military duty had been, and, at times, she saw that far away stare and the momentary flight from reality that was a trademark of many veterans. Now she saw true contentment in his eyes, and that pleased her. She smiled at him and gave him a "thumbs up" sign.

Turning east from Kineo, Ken headed for Greenville and lifted slightly to turn above the village proper before landing in a plume of water close to Folsom's Air Service. He cut the engines and drifted close to the dock so that he could refuel the plane. Don quickly jumped onto the dock and ran to the office. He returned in a few minutes to tell Ken that he had made arrangements for a charter flight back to New York.

"I was hoping to have you as a guest for a few days." Ken sounded disappointed. "Do we have time for a lunch before you leave?"

"That sounds good to me, Ken. I'll take a rain check on my visit. I've got a lot of things going right now. I've just completed a contract with a construction company to run shuttles to and from an aluminum plant under construction in Quebec," Don told him apologetically.

Jean had been listening to the conversation with interest. "If you don't mind my asking, Mr. Poole, is the company's name Finch Construction Company?"

"Why yes," he replied.

144

"That's my father's company. I knew that he was negotiating with a Canadian firm, but was not sure that he had received the bid."

"As far as I know, it's a go," Don answered. "I can't tell you how pleased I am to work with your father, Mr. Finch."

"I'm glad to hear that."

"I knew there was something special about you, Mrs. Mackenzie. Your father is my kind of man. He told me that he wanted performance without excuses, and if he got it he'd pay any reasonable price. I'm not bragging, but I think he'll find us to be the best, and if we're not, I'll damn well find out why." There was enthusiasm about him that was contagious. Jean approved of her father's choice.

"This sounds like a time for a celebration for all of us," Ken exclaimed. "We can walk to the restaurant from here. Lori and I always eat at this one on the waterfront."

During the course of ordering and eating lunch, Don and Jean learned that they both knew several people in the Lake George – Albany area. Don asked a lot of questions about her father's business, and by the time the meal was over Don was obviously pleased to have made her acquaintance. He insisted on paying for lunch before returning to the air service landing.

"Thank you, Don, for locating a plane that fits our corporate needs at this time. I can't tell you how much I've missed flying. I do a little bit at our Reserve meetings, but I like it better when I can fill my log book with a lot more hours. Best of luck on your new business venture. I appreciate the offer to join you as a partner. I'm honored really, but I'm satisfied with what I'm doing now at Great Northern. So long, friend. Remember, the welcome mat is always out for you."

Touched by Ken's words, the two men embraced in a bear hug. "It's been a pleasure, Ken. And it has also been a nice surprise to meet you, Mrs. Mackenzie. I'm sure we'll meet again."

Jean shook his hand and told him, "I have kept the Mackenzie name until my divorce is final, but after that I'll reclaim my own."

"It's been a pleasure, Ma'am."

Don kneeled down to Lori and hugged her, "You take good care of your daddy; he's one of the best."

She mumbled good-bye to him.

Later that same evening, Ken tucked Lori into bed and retired to the deck. It was a beautiful evening. Just before Jean left for her cabin they had discussed Don's sister. Jean did not know her, but knew her husband, Captain Hal Charles. He was a very popular native of Glens Falls. The town placed a granite obelisk with a bronze marker in one of their parks to pay tribute to him and to honor his death at Bataan. Ken had thought it strange that Don did not once mention his sister whom he must have been close to. He had taught her how to fly, and she was a good student. He could attest to that. Perhaps her death at the hands of the Germans was still too painful to talk about.

He sat in one of the Adirondack chairs and studied the stars, unconsciously locating the North Star. Both Lorraine and Lea were attracted to the star and the symbolism that's associated with it. That night he focused on it for a long time. He had the strongest feeling that there was something significant in the way he felt. The memory of Lea in North Africa was still capable of producing tears. At the far end of Savage Pond, a loon called into the night, sending its hauntingly melancholic message across the water. The call was answered from several points around the pond, creating a cacophony of sound that never failed to make him feel sad and melancholic.

Ever since the war's end, Ken had driven himself to fill his life with activity. He had successfully established himself at the Great Northern Paper Company as a forester in charge of harvesting operations in the vast spruce-fir forests of the northeast. At the same time he had been building the cabin they lived in. It was close to his work. He dropped Lori off every work day at a neighbor's place in Kokadjo. Jean insisted that she take care of Lori while she was in the area. He was happy with the arrangement. After Lori started school, she was able to catch a bus at Kokadjo which took her and a few other children to Greenville.

146

Working and caring for Lori had become his life, and he was thankful for the ability to do so. She made each day worthwhile, filling his life with purpose and joy. The next few days after Don had delivered the airplane, he took Lori and Jean for a ride up to the Rippogenus Dam. They found it fascinating to watch the pulpwood flow over the spillway down the sluiceway to the paper mill at Millinocket a few miles away.

He made it a routine every time he took the plane into the air to report in to Greenville Dispatch, who monitored all messages passing through the area. His Grumman amphibian became Blue Goose One when Ken was at the controls. He also reported in when he had arrived at his destination, and on that day, as Lori and Jean were exiting the plane, an urgent call came over the speaker.

"We have a mayday signal from a plane experiencing engine failure. Repeat: Mayday, plane down on azimuth of twelve degrees somewhere along the Allagash River. Plane's transponder is sending out homing signal."

"Greenville Dispatch, this is Blue Goose One, responding to call for help. I will immediately be airborne and enroute. My ETA (estimated time of arrival) is thirty-five minutes. I repeat: this is Blue Goose One responding to Mayday call."

He told Lori and Jean that he did not know how long this was going to take, and waved as he began to lift off, heading north with the two Pratt and Whitney engines running wide open. A plane down was serious business in the North Woods, and the brotherhood of fliers who braved the wilderness skies took it as a privilege to respond to any call for help, for they could be the next ones in trouble. The area had some of the best "seat of their pants" pilots in the world, and it was a close-knit band of professionals. The call worried Ken, for generally a forced landing was not a forgiving incident.

Ken turned his receiving instrument on so that he could pick up the transponder's signal. He had it, but it was very weak. "Blue Goose One, this is Greenville Dispatch. The downed plane is owned by Don's Air Service out of Lake George, New York."

"Blue Goose One to dispatch, I read you loud and clear. Dispatch, please call Don Poole at his office to let them know that he has a plane down. I'm on track to down plane and will call when I have a sighting. Out."

"Roger, Blue Goose One. Making call to Donovan Poole."

Traveling at 200 miles per hour, Ken made it to the approximate vicinity of the crash site in a very short period of time. He had enough fuel on board to make the round trip without a problem. He turned to the radio frequency commonly used by pilots in the area and was picking up some erratic signals over the speaker. The messages were unclear, but the desperation came through despite the faulty air waves. He did understand that the plane's call signal was "Angel."

"This is Blue Goose One responding to Mayday call, can you read me, Angel? Do you read me, Angel?"

"Angel to Blue Goose. I read you loud and clear. My engine quit, and my battery is low. I am down on Round Pond."

"Blue Goose to Angel, I am minutes away from you. Do not use your radio anymore; save your battery. Out."

Ken picked up the Allagash River past Lake Chamberlain and Eagle Lake. It was a rugged region of wilderness with endless miles of forest and waterways without any roadways. The region was famous for its pristine beauty, but in reality it had been used for generations by the Great Northern for the production of spruce and fir logs and pulpwood. The further he pushed the Grumman northward, the stronger the distress signal became. He was making progress. The river made a sharp turn to the east at one point where Ken decided to save time, proceeding in a straight line to pick up the river ahead of him. The signals became weaker, so he turned east and followed the dog leg bend of the river to what was known as Round Pond. He was at the edge of the pond and scouted the southern perimeter, finding nothing.

Turning north he slowed down to observe the pond's shore for any sign of the plane. He knew he was close to it. Suddenly at the extreme northern end of the wider body of water, he spotted a red and white Norseman plane in the water. He speeded up and made a turn low over the craft to see what was happening. He saw a lone figure slumped over one of the pontoons beneath the pilot's door. Without hesitation Ken brought the plane down as close to the craft as possible, intending to stop on the port side of the Norseman.

He instantly called dispatch to report his sighting and jumped into the water. Ken swam to the injured pilot. As he approached the body, he was surprised to see that it was a woman. "Are you all right?" he asked. The water was about four feet deep, so he was able to stand up. The woman evidently had been talking on the radio because the microphone was dangling out from the door. She was slumped partly over the pontoon and half in the water. He noticed some blood puddling in the water and was alarmed. The only course available for him was to lift her out of the water off the pontoon and carry her to the Grumman.

First he reached for a pulse on her wrist. She was at least alive. He turned her head towards him and got the surprise of his life. He was staring into the face of Lieutenant Lea Charles!

Chapter Sixteen

Ken worried about moving Lea Charles in case she had internal injuries, but there was no other way to get her into the safety of the aircraft. He carefully balanced her body in his two arms holding her above the water. She was soaking wet from head to toe. He walked slowly toward the Grumman, still cradling her in his arms, and reached up with his right hand to open the access door to the rear of the plane. He leaned through the door and laid her in the center of the aisle between the seats. Then he quickly opened the exterior hatch to grab the blankets and pillows he always carried in case of an emergency.

With as little disturbance as possible, he wrapped the blankets about her wet body to prevent shock and placed a pillow under her head. Ripping the first aid kit off the back of the pilot seat, he took clean cotton balls and swabbed the bleeding wound on her head, rinsing it with hydrogen peroxide. The wound bubbled and foamed, indicating the presence of some infection. He tilted her head to one side so that it would not get into her eyes. She opened her eyes and began to cry.

"Lea Charles, can you hear me?" Ken whispered in her ear. She moved her head. "Do you have any injuries that I don't see?"

"My head hurts," she mumbled almost inaudibly.

"Listen, you've had an accident, and I'm going to fly you out of here to a hospital." He took her two hands in his. They were cold and unresponsive, and she began to shake all over. "You hold on, Lea Charles."

He slipped into the pilot's seat, started the engine and rammed the throttles forward for a takeoff, switching the heaters on full. As he was getting airborne, he called Greenville Dispatch. "I have the pilot from 'Angel' on board. She's injured, and I want you to alert Greenville Hospital that I will be landing at the large wharf across from the hospital. She may be going into shock, and there's nothing I can do except get her to Greenville as soon as possible. I'm twenty minutes away. Have emergency team meet me at the landing."

"Lea Charles, if you can hear me, is there anything that the hospital should be alerted about?" He watched her in his rear view mirror and saw her wipe her forehead.

"It's just my head. I hit the windshield…"

"Okay, Lea, lie still; it won't be long."

Fifteen minutes later he entered Greenville air space at full speed and hit the water at a low angle, heading straight at the wharf where he saw nurses and a Greenville Fire Department ambulance backed up to the landing. He opened his door and threw a rope at the closest fireman to secure the craft to the dock. "She's on the floor in the back." He pointed behind him. A minute later she was being loaded into the ambulance on her way to the hospital.

Relieved that she was getting care, Ken taxied over to Folsom's and refueled the Grumman. A call to Don's office was in order, and he went into the office to place the call and pay for his fuel.

Don answered the phone as if he was expecting it. "Hello, this is Don Poole."

"Don, this is Ken Morgan. I'm calling to let you know that your sister is in the Greenville Hospital. I just brought her in. Don't be alarmed; she has a nasty bang on her head, and other than the trauma of the accident, she appears to be all right. She was able to communicate with me, so be thankful for that."

"Thank God. I didn't want her to make the trip, but she insisted that she'd be fine. That plane just had an engine rebuild; I don't understand it."

"You may be interested in knowing that her skill as a pilot and her guts to do what has to be done probably saved her

151

from a more devastating tragedy. She made a perfect landing in a very small pool of water and at the last minute hit either a rock or a log which crumpled the right float. The plane seems to be intact except for the float."

"Ken, I can't tell you how relieved I am to receive your call. Thanks, friend. I'm coming to Greenville to see Lea and to salvage the plane."

"I've got a question that has been on my mind ever since I saw your sister at the crash site. I had met her several times during the war, and I was led to believe that she was killed in a dog fight with German fighters. She's a very special flier. I know that she flew with you before the war."

"My sister Lea is a very special person in many ways, Ken. I gave her the 'Angel' designation because it fit her. Yes, she tangled with two 109's and shot one of them down. She was hit and crashed in enemy territory where the Luftwaffe took her prisoner. For all the hatred I have for the Germans, I have to say that they treated her fairly and notified the Red Cross that she was their prisoner. She lives with her son at Diamond Point on Lake George. I never knew that you and Lea had met," Don explained.

"Please, when you come to Greenville, stay at my place. I have a Studebaker coupe and a Willys-Overland four wheel drive pickup at your disposal. Be my guest; it will be a pleasure."

"Thanks, Ken. I really appreciate your offer... Say, would you mind if I brought along Lea's son? He's a joy to his uncle. Lea is a wonderful mother to him."

"I would expect that of her, Don. Please, bring her son. We'll be looking forward to your visit. Now don't worry about your sister. She's in good hands."

He went to the Grumman and removed his khaki flight coverall and slipped into a pair of pants. His socks and shoes had already dried out. He wanted to look reasonably respectable to visit Lea at the hospital before he left for Savage Pond. He stopped to kill some time at his favorite restaurant so that the staff would be able to take care of Lea before he visited her. He had a hamburger, a piece of custard pie and a couple cups of coffee. On his way to the hospital he passed a florist and stopped to get a dozen red roses. The card read, "To a lovely lady from a friend."

The nurse at the reception desk recognized him and took a vase from a closet for the flowers. "Our patient is resting. The doctor is finished with her." She pointed to a private room down the corridor on the south side of the hospital that filled the room with sunshine. There was a nice view of Squaw Mountain in the distance. Ken placed the flowers on her bedside stand and quietly leaned over her.

"Hello, Lea."

She turned her head and saw him standing beside her. "Hello, Major Morgan. It's a small world, isn't it? We seem to meet under unusual circumstances. Thank you for answering my call for help."

"I'm thankful that I was able to respond. Pilots have that obligation. I didn't know that it was you until I arrived on scene."

"I had a feeling that it was you, hearing our radio conversation. My God, I was so scared." He took her hands in his and squeezed them. Tears formed in the corner of her dark eyes.

"You set that Norseman down in the only available spot for miles around, displaying remarkably good judgment and an above average amount of skill in doing so. Don't blame yourself for what happened. Your brother and your son are probably on their way here as we speak."

She turned her head away and wiped the tears. "Don didn't want me to take the trip, but I insisted."

"Don told me that, too, but listen, Lea, the plane is only superficially damaged. The cargo is intact, and you survived a crash landing in a vast wilderness environment. I'd say that the gods were on your side today."

"I hit a log that busted the float in two. As soon as I landed, I took the two life preservers that were in the plane and wrapped them around the broken float and inflated them with the emergency can of air on each. They lifted the plane slightly, and hopefully they will keep it from sinking any more."

Ken chuckled at her ingenuity and determination. "I'll bet you slipped those life preservers on before you called for help."

"I didn't want the plane to go into the water any more than it had. I did call right after. I was standing on the pilot side pontoon using the radio when I was talking to you. All I know is that everything went black after that. I hit my head on the windshield when the float hit an obstacle and pivoted me around."

Ken drew up a chair to be closer to hear her, and so that she could see him easier. She saw the flowers, and a smile crossed her lips. "Thank you for the flowers. It's been a long time since someone brought me flowers..." She dropped off to sleep in mid-sentence.

Ken bent over her to make sure she was breathing normal. He squeezed her hand and left the room. The nurse told him that she would probably be sleeping through the night. The doctor had given her a light sedative. He thanked her and headed for Savage Pond. The sun was approaching the horizon as he landed and taxied to the dock. Lori and Jean caught the ropes and secured the plane. He was glad to be home - it had been quite a day, and he was tired.

The three had a supper of fresh salmon and topped it off with a jelly donut and cocoa. They noticed that Ken was not in a talkative mood. He briefly described what had taken place and kept his thoughts to himself. He tucked Lori in bed for the night and walked out onto the deck, taking a seat in one of the Adirondack chairs beside Jean.

"It was nice of you to take care of Lori for me, Jean. I appreciate that. Your soon-to-be ex-husband was a pilot, and maybe you can understand how personal Mayday calls are for pilots. To respond to an emergency becomes a duty to the brotherhood if you can call it that."

"The fact that you take your role as a pilot so seriously is one of the reasons that makes you such a special one, Ken. How badly is Don Poole's plane damaged?"

"It could be worse. He'll probably have to replace the float and struts. The engine could be the most expensive. At this point we don't know why it failed. It could be fuel, electrical or mechanical failure. His sister showed a lot of grit landing such a heavy aircraft as that Norseman on such a small body of water."

"The way you say her name tells me that she has won your respect," Jean had observed. She regretted the statement as soon as she said it.

"Is it that obvious?" he asked without elaboration.

She knew that he wanted to be alone and stood up. "Well, it's getting late."

Ken started to stand when Jean placed her two hands on his shoulders, holding him down. "I know my way home, Ken. You look exhausted, so rest well." She bent over him and boldly kissed him on the lips. Goodnight, Ken."

"Goodnight, Jean."

For the rest of the evening Ken thought of Lea lying on the white sheets in the hospital, and then he could not ignore the fact that Jean's kiss opened up a whole new world that did nothing but confuse him.

The next morning, Ken and Lori had just finished breakfast of French toast and bacon when a plane landed and aimed straight for their dock. They ran outside to see Don taxiing toward them in a Norseman single engine float plane. They caught the ropes and secured the craft. Ken was glad to see Don and was not surprised by his visit. "I thought you brought your nephew up with you, Don."

"I did, but he wanted to stay with his mother this morning. To be real honest, after I saw how good Lea was doing, I was anxious to take a look at her plane. Do you have the time to show me where it is?"

"I half expected you this morning," Ken grinned. "Sure, I'm ready to go. Do you mind if we take Lori with us? She's out of school now."

"I didn't even think of that," Don shook his head. "Sure, we've got plenty of room. These Norsemans are thirsty, but

155

they can tote a heavy load with ease. I'm impressed with them."

Ken told Lori to get her light jacket and her heavy sneakers for the trip. She was anxious to accompany them and climbed into one of the rear seats and buckled up. He nodded his approval to her and released the tethering ropes, pushing the plane away from the dock.

Don started the engine and took off as soon as Ken fastened his safety belt. Ken gave him directions to the site. When they arrived at Round Pond, Don came down low to skim the water, looking for logs or driftwood in the landing path. Then he made a sharp turn to port and set the Norseman down, coming up close to the crippled aircraft so that he and Ken could step from their pontoon to the downed plane's whole pontoon. Ken quickly climbed out to tie the two crafts together with a small line taken from a pocket on the plane's door.

They both checked the broken float and strut and observed that Lea's resourceful use of the two life preservers was still holding the plane from sinking. Don climbed out on the end of the good pontoon to lift the engine cover, anxious to see if he could determine what made the engine fail. A few seconds later Ken heard him curse to himself and asked:

"Did you find something, Don?"

"I can't believe such stupidity," Don replied. "One of the gas fittings was loose, leaking gas all over the engine. It's a miracle the plane didn't go up in flames on Lea. Can you check to see if there is any life left in the batteries, Ken?"

"Sure," Ken replied, climbing into the pilot's seat and turned on the ignition. "Both gas tanks are empty, Don. She must have switched, thinking that was her problem. Stand clear, let me see if the battery has any life left."

Checking to see that Don pulled himself away from the open engine cover, Ken activated the starter long enough to determine that there was enough life to start the engine if it had fuel. Don put into words what they both were thinking.

"I'm amazed what little work needs to be done to the plane. Folsom will be able to handle it. I wouldn't be surprised if they even have a float in stock. How about if we load up with a portion of the load and deliver it? I'm full of fuel. It's at a plant site about two hundred miles north of here."

"Well, let's get at it, Don. If we take all we can from the starboard side, it will make things a lot easier for the repair crew when they come to fix the plane."

In order to distribute the load in the Norseman so that it was secure, Ken suggested that they fold up the passenger seats. He would hold Lori in his lap for the trip north. A half hour later, they had two-thirds of the canned beans, tomatoes, and peaches loaded and tied down in Don's plane, and they were flying north. Ken told Lori that she was going to pass over the International Boundary between Canada and the United States.

The load was delivered without incident, and they instantly returned to Greenville where Don refueled the plane at Folsom's. They walked to the hospital to see how Lea was doing, finding her sitting up in bed. She looked up and smiled at them as they entered the room. Her forehead was bandaged. She had combed her black hair. Ken noted that she had a few strands of gray which were becoming to her. A young boy of about nine years of age was sitting beside her bed.

"How's my baby sister doing?" Don asked, kissing her on the top of her head.

She gave him a questioning look. "How bad is the plane?"

"The plane is in better shape than I imagined. All it will need is a float and maybe a strut," Ken was pleased to tell her. "Your engine failed from a defective gas line."

Lea turned to Ken. "Hello Ken, I'll bet that this little girl with you is Lori. I have never met you before, Lori, but I knew how important you were to your Dad. This is my son, Donald, who just got promoted to the fifth grade."

"Lori and I are pleased to meet you, Donald," Ken extended his hand to the slender dark-eyed boy.

Lori looked up at him and shyly said, "Hi."

"Hi, Lori," he said, looking up at Ken with a serious look. "My mother told me that you are the one who found her and brought her to the hospital. We were scared when Uncle Don and I learned that she had crashed. Thank you for helping her."

"I did what any other pilot in the vicinity would have done, Donald, and I appreciate your concern for your mother. She's a very brave and resourceful lady. I'm glad to see more color in her cheeks today," Ken replied.

Don told her about the partial load they delivered to the plant, and that Folsom was going to take on the task of repairing the plane. Ken added that her brother was coming back to Savage Pond to stay for as long as he likes. "How soon are they going to discharge you, Lea?"

"The doctor was just in. He told me that I could leave today. In another two days I could stop by the out-patient clinic to have the bandage changed. I'm a little sore from the rough landing, but other than that I'm fine."

Ken looked at the people around the room and announced in a happy mood, "Why don't we get you discharged? Then you can come up to the cabin with us. Lori and I have plenty of room for all of you. We have two extra rooms upstairs for guests, and Donald can use the loft that overhangs the great room. It's a fun place to sleep, and the feather mattress is like sleeping on a cloud."

Donald smiled at Ken's description of the loft. "I'd like that!" he exclaimed, looking at his mother.

"Your offer of hospitality is appreciated and graciously accepted, Ken. Thank you. To be real honest, I'm anxious to get out of this hospital bed," she explained.

"You're going to have a full house, Ken," Don commented, pleased that they could all be together.

"I think it will be great," Ken assured them. Then, he saw a detached look come over Lea's face.

Lea spoke hesitantly in a low voice and with a slight tremor, "I have a question to ask you, Ken, because I have a feeling you may not know."

"Know what, Lea?"

"Did you notice anything about me when you lifted me from my plane to yours?"

"Only that you had a gash on your forehead. What are you talking about?" he asked.

"When I was shot down, my foot and the lower part of my leg was severely damaged. The German doctors removed it. I have an artificial leg. I use a cane to help me get around."

Chapter Seventeen

Lea's mention of her misfortune was an issue that she had spent long hours trying to reconcile the fact that she was no longer complete and might be characterized by some as a cripple, or even worse, a freak. It was not the physical loss of her leg that bothered her as much as the perception of others. Once she accepted it as a fact of life, she was determined to not let it diminish her ability to fly a plane or drive an automobile. One year after the war, she received her license for both vehicles. It was the crowning achievement of her life.

Ken had not noticed anything different with Lea when he brought her to the hospital. He listened to her talk about the prosthetic leg she now wore with a certain amount of indifference. The fact that she did or did not have an artificial leg had nothing to do with his respect and admiration of her.

"My reaction to your loss is not pity or sympathy, Lea. When I first saw you in the Norseman unconscious, my initial thought was that you may have been a cousin or even a sister who looked like you. For years I had believed you to be dead after word came of your being shot down by the Germans. I was angry at those who had placed you in harm's way, and I mourned your loss even though we had met for such a brief time. You had become my friend, and I missed you. It was just that simple. Then I realized that it was you out there in the wilderness, and I rejoiced in that fact. You have risen above your tragedy, and I'm so proud of your courage." He had spoken from the heart, and he had spoken the truth.

Lea studied him and listened carefully to his words and understood what he was saying. "I'm glad that it was you who found me. The radio reception was terrible, and the moment that I recognized your voice, I knew everything was going to be all right. My last thought before losing consciousness was about you and *Sweet Lori*." A moist film clouded her eyes, and she turned away from those around her bed. "Would you please tell the nurse at the duty station that I'm going with you? And please, wait for me in the lounge."

Ken squeezed her hand and followed the others out of the room. Don was the first to speak: "I never knew that you and Lea had met during the war. I swear I never knew, Ken."

"I believe you, Don. We fleetingly met several times on our way to and from Europe and North Africa. I admired her flying skills which she said were developed with her big brother when he was hauling the United States Mail."

Don was amused at the turn of events. "She did like to tag along with me. She was a little bit of a tomboy and took to flying as if it was the most natural thing in the world. Her instincts at the controls of an aircraft are greater than anyone I know. While we're waiting for the staff to release her, I should make a call to Matt Colson," Don told them, looking down the hallway for a phone booth.

Ten minutes later, Don entered the waiting lounge and sat down beside Ken. "There, I had promised Matt that I'd let him know how Lea was."

"Who's this Matt Colson?" Ken asked innocently.

"He's Lea's fiancée. They're engaged to marry," Don replied.

The words struck Ken like a physical blow. Suddenly his vision of the future was turned upside down. He had no right to make assumptions about his relationship with Lea. His feelings for her had been built in that chaotic crucible of the war when nothing was forever. He knew that better than anyone, yet he had not considered the fact that Lea was in control of her life, not him. To have picked up four years after their last visit in North Africa was denying reality that had just hit him in the face.

Lori noticed something was bothering him. "What's wrong, Daddy?"

He felt vulnerable and emotionally naked to the prying eyes of his companions, and walked to the window and stared at the shoreline. "It's nothing, Honey. I was just thinking how things had been... Sometimes we spend too much time in the past when we should be looking to the future."

Don perceived the source of his discomfort and stood by his side. "I thought you knew, Ken. I should have told you sooner."

"No, Don, you had no obligation to inform me of Lea's affairs. I'm a stranger to both of you. My folks and Lorraine frequently told me to look forward instead of backward. They were correct. I think I needed something to break me loose from the ties the past have on me. I had hoped and assumed when I should have known better. I had no right to act upon those fantasies we all had while the war was on. I admit that I clung to them, no matter how unreasonable they were, but I was wrong..."

Don placed an arm around his friend's shoulders. "You were not alone with your dreams, Ken. At one time or another, we were all little boys and scared of the dark."

"I've been letting my admiration and respect for Lea creep beyond the bounds of reason. I should have known better, but I can handle it."

Lea was wheeled into the waiting lounge by the nurse who said that she had to be wheeled out from the hospital. "If you wish, you may borrow the chair for a few days. Our patient is still a little weak and should not overdo."

"Thank you, nurse. The use of the chair is a good idea for today anyway," Don agreed, noticing that she had a new cane with her on the chair.

Lea saw the angst in Ken's face and was about to speak when Ken suggested, "What do you say if we eat here in town before returning to the cabin? I mention that and insist on picking up the tab. It isn't every day that our lives are brightened up by old friends. Lori and I are looking forward to playing host; besides, we're anxious to show off our new log cabin on Savage Pond." He finished and avoided making eye contact with Lea.

Don agreed to push Lea's chair to the waterfront restaurant where they were all seated near a window with a view of Moosehead Lake. They could also see Don's Norseman tied up at Folsom's. After they had ordered dinner, Don told his sister that he had called Matt Colson and informed him of what happened.

Ken was glad that Don brought up the subject. "Congratulations on your engagement, Lea. He's a very lucky man, and I wish you all the best."

Lea smiled at him and said, "Thanks, Ken. It's nice to have friends that care. Matt and I met at a hospital shortly after my release from the German POW camp. He's also from a small town close to Diamond Point, so we have a lot in common."

"I'm happy for you."

Later that night, after Lori and Donald had been tucked into bed, the three adults went out on the deck to enjoy a beautiful evening with a soft breeze blowing from the northwest. In the silence of the night they could hear the gentle lap of the water against the rocks. It was a soothing sound that Ken never tired of. The snap of a branch broke the reverie of the night, and Ken saw a flashlight flickering on the shoreline.

"Hello, is anyone at home?" Jean called softly from the darkness.

"Come up on the porch, Jean," Ken invited her, pulling a chair closer to include her in the circle. "You've already met my friend Don Poole, and this lady beside me is his sister, Lea Charles. She's the lady who survived the crash. This is our neighbor, Jean Mackenzie. We're the only two cabins on the lake, and hopefully it will stay that way."

"Hi again, Mrs. Mackenzie," Don said, pleased to see her.

"Welcome to Savage Pond. It's good to see you again, Mr. Poole, and I'm especially pleased to meet the lady pilot that Ken has told me about. My ex-husband was a pilot. I didn't mean to interrupt your evening together, but I wanted to let you know that I'm leaving in the morning, Ken. My father told me that an owner of one of my homes wants to make some major changes, and I really need to check out those modifications."

Ken added, "Jean is an architect and works in her father's company, which just happens to be the firm that has awarded Don a contract. It's a small world."

Lea caught a glimpse of Jean in the rays of light coming from the great room in the cabin, noting her slender figure and blonde hair. There was a reserved air about the newcomer that projected her unpretentiousness. "I'm also pleased to meet you, Mrs. Mackenzie."

"Please call me Jean. These Maine woods have a way of making all of us neighbors, and the formality of titles are out of place."

They talked a lot that evening about the company Jean's father owned and about projects that might be on the planning table. They found that Jean was a well-informed partner in the enterprise, but insisted that she was simply acting as consultant. Lea and Don retired early and left Jean and Ken alone on the deck.

"I'm glad to have a chance to speak to you alone before I leave, Ken. I want you to know that I've enjoyed our friendship, and I don't want to have anything interfere with it. I understand your position with Lea. She's a lovely lady, and I like her. What I'm trying to say, and am saying it badly, is that ever since I jumped out of Lauren's plane and found my way to your cabin, I've frequently thought of the incident. I understand that it would be wrong to read too much in what happened, but it's been bothering me a lot. I'm not the socialite flighty stereotype that some suppose me to be. I like straight talk."

"I know you do, Jean."

She hesitated several seconds and bluntly asked, "Would I be wasting my time thinking that there might be something between us, or am I simply letting an infatuation run away with my better judgment? Please, I beg of you, be honest with me."

Surprised by her direct request, Ken did not hesitate. "Jean, you continue to amaze me, and I admit that your friendship is important to me. I understand what you're asking of me, and you deserve a straight answer. We're really strangers to each other, but trust and friendship are good foundations to build a relationship on. Beyond that, I cannot tell you what my true feelings are. To be truthful, I really don't know myself. Many things have taken place in my life that have hurt and been disappointing, and I want to limit those incidents. I want more out of life, and I have to settle that in my heart before I commit to a relationship that has no future. For the time being, would you be satisfied to know that I consider you a lovely caring person whom I enjoy being with? I'll miss you, Jean. When are you coming back?"

"I won't be long, Ken. Thank you for your honesty. Good night, friend," she said, standing up from the chair. "I'll find my own way back."

Ken watched her slowly walk across the deck with hesitant steps. Then, she turned and rushed to him with open arms. They embraced there in the soft solitude of the night. She lifted her lips to his and spoke in a soft voice. "Thank you for coming into my life. I've been so lonely all these years."

Without another word, she was gone. Ken stood watching the North Star that guided her back to her cabin, wondering if what had just taken place was significant. Why did he hold the infatuation so long for Lea? He had often thought that it was one of those war-time incidents that only had meaning while the war was taking place, yet he continued to nourish it even after word of Lea's death. That had to be significant, but it only led to disappointment. He had completely misread her feelings towards him, and just maybe, he had perverted the semantics of friendship. All he was certain of now was that the knowledge of Lea's engagement had stung him deeply. It hurt, and it angered him that he was never given a chance to declare himself. It wasn't fair. All during the war years, he was vulnerable to anything that made his life more enjoyable. And, finally, perhaps he was more fickle than he had imagined; he had fantasized the relationship instead of seeing it as it really was — an acquaintance.

The next morning, Ken was up before dawn preparing breakfast for his guests. He made up a pancake batter, broiled sausages and a full pot of coffee. In case they wanted a simpler breakfast, he also had cornflakes and bananas.

Don was the first to rise. Ken quietly indicated that the bathroom was free for now. By the time Don had showered and shaved, Ken had built up a stack of pancakes and served them on the table near the front entrance.

"I envy you, Ken. This log cabin just wreaks of warmth and personality. Thanks for being such a gracious host. I'm not used to being served like this."

"It's a pleasure having friends. At times it can get a little lonely up here, but I was desperate for the opportunity to get my life in order since the war. This place has been wonderful therapy for me and Lori. It has brought us closer together. What are your plans, Don?" Ken asked, taking a seat opposite his guest and pouring coffee for the two of them.

"I'm heading back to New York to check out a helicopter. What are your thoughts about its future in aviation, Ken?"

Ken finished chewing a sausage and said, "I had an interesting talk with a Coast Guard officer at one of our reserve meetings recently. They are enthused with the potential for search and rescue operations which they perform on an hourly basis. This officer was qualified to fly one, and he said it was a tricky operation especially under severe weather conditions. He told me that the Army and the Air Force are conducting evaluation exercises. My guess is that we're going to see a lot more of them in the future."

"I've had similar thoughts. I knew that the Coast Guard had requested several models from various manufacturers. I've got an appointment with a Bell sales representative. I'll keep you posted on events," Don said, pushing his empty plate away. "If I was to eat like this every day I'd be overweight. I'm going down to the plane to see if I can reach anyone on the radio. Maybe I can dictate an oral flight plan with Folsom. Thanks, Ken."

Several minutes after Don left the kitchen, Lea opened the door of her room and entered the great room. "Good morning,

Ken. I slept like a log all night. It's so peaceful and quiet up here."

"Good morning, Lea. The bathroom is free. Don has already gone down to the plane to see if he can roust anyone on the radio. Reception is usually pretty good here on Savage Pond. The two kids are still sleeping. This morning I'm the chef. May I fix you some blueberry pancakes?"

"I love them, but my limit is two, please. The cabin is beautiful. I won't be long," she said.

"Take your time."

Ken sat down and poured himself another cup of coffee, waiting for Lea to appear before he did more pancakes. He saw Donald climbing down from the loft. "Did you sleep well, Donald?"

"Yes, Mr. Morgan. What a neat place this is. I heard the loons for the first time. It was kind of sad to hear them. They made me feel lonely."

"They can make one feel sad and melancholic. It's an ancient call that has not changed down through the ages. The fact that the birds have survived unchanged for so long is a tribute to their instincts for survival. They over- winter on the Atlantic Ocean. Wolves, foxes, and owls own the night up here in the northern woods. Now, your mother is occupying the bathroom, so I can get you breakfast. I have pancakes with real maple syrup and sausage or cereals, take your pick." Ken offered him.

"Pancakes would be great."

"Just take a seat at the table, and they'll be coming right up. How about some milk? You're a little young for coffee, but I was drinking it occasionally at your age," Ken chuckled at him.

"That will be fine." Ken liked the boy's good manners.

Lea came out of the bathroom and took a seat at the table beside her son. "How did you sleep, Donald?"

"Great, Mom. Did you hear the loons last night?"

"Yes," she answered, watching Ken serve them pancakes.

"Your brother said that he had an appointment with a helicopter representative. Have you ever flown in one?"

"No, have you?"

"I tried one out with a Coast Guard officer a month ago at Reserves. They certainly have their place within the aviation industry."

"Thanks for breakfast, Mr. Morgan," Donald said, excusing himself from the table.

Lea finished her pancakes in silence and looked around the great room in the sunshine. She saw a large piece of furniture in the corner covered with a dust cloth. "Is that a piano in the corner over there?" Lea pointed.

"Yes, Lori keeps it covered so that she won't have to dust it every day," Ken grinned. "She takes lessons from a local lady every week. "I remember that you played very well, Lea. Would you please play something?"

"Oh, I haven't played for years," she answered, slowly walking over to the instrument.

Ken removed the dust cover for her and pulled out the bench. "Lori and her teacher both say that it's in good tune. It belonged to my wife, Lorraine."

She sat down on the bench and lifted the keyboard cover. She flexed her fingers, ran through the scale, then began to play the most popular song of the war, *I'll Be Seeing You In All The Old Familiar Places,* as sung by Vera Lynn. It had been three years since Ken had heard the song, yet it still had the power to emotionally transport him back to England, remembering how it was. A moist film covered his eyes. That same old feeling of being alone embraced him. He could not believe that Lea was here in his cabin playing the piano. It seemed like a dream. She continued and played a medley of several songs before turning to confront him.

"It brings back memories, doesn't it?" she asked in a soft voice.

He turned his back to her, acting busy with the stove, "Ya, it strikes some sensitive chords all right. You play very well. Music has a way of setting moods and triggering suppressed thoughts. I'd almost forgotten how it had been. It seems so long ago."

She left the piano and stood by his side placing her hand on his arm. "Please, Lea, I thought I had put all of that behind me, but I was wrong, I was wrong..."

"Can we still remain friends, Ken? I want that very much," she cried, seeing the hurt in his eyes.

"Sure, I'll settle for that," Ken answered in a wavering voice. "You should know that I wanted more, but that's impossible now. I don't blame you. We have to take happiness wherever we find it. I truly wish you all the happiness you deserve."

Lea grasped his hand, "I pray that things work out for you..."

Before she could finish, Don rushed into the cabin in an excited state. "I hate to eat and run, Ken, but I've got an important meeting scheduled at home in New York. Lea, get Donnie ready, I'm anxious to get airborne. We've got good weather all across the northeast."

Ten minutes later, Ken and Lori were waving good-bye to their guests as the Norseman lifted off the water and set a course due west.

Chapter Eighteen

Two Years Later – June 25, 1950

Ken had just returned from work and picked up Lori from the family in Kokadjo who kept her after school. It had been a long hard day, and he was tired from checking harvest operations. The minute he and Lori entered the house the phone rang.

"Hello," he answered.

"Colonel Morgan, this is Brigadier General Hobbs at Headquarters, Dover Foxcroft. Have you heard the news?"

"No Sir, I've been in the field all day. Is something wrong?"

"The North Koreans have just smashed through the 38th Parallel with tanks and an overpowering force. The South Koreans are reeling under the assault. Our unit has been activated. I'm calling to give you verbal orders to report to Headquarters within twenty-four hours. I know how demanding that order is for you, but it's imperative that we start every functioning squadron on its way to Korea. As it is we may be too late, but MacArthur has promised that we will hold the southern tip of the peninsula. I'm sorry, Colonel, but that's what we're up against."

Ken swallowed hard. "I understand the situation, Sir. It looks like another example of unpreparedness."

"You said it, Colonel. Good luck."

"Thank you, Sir."

Ken sat down at the kitchen table to collect his thoughts. Twenty-four hours was not much time to place Lori and close down his home. The Great Northern was prepared to release him on a short notice. He had called there first to notify them of his imminent departure.

Lori saw how the call was distressing him. Ken turned to her. "Lori, do you remember how we have talked several times about the possibility of Daddy having to leave if he is ordered by the Air Force Reserve he had joined?"

"I remember, Daddy. Today we learned that there was an attack against a friendly country called South Korea. We found it on the globe in our classroom. Does that mean that you'll have to go and fight in a war?"

"Yes, it does mean that, Honey, and there's nothing I can do about it. Are you prepared to go to Grandpop's and Grandmother's while I do my duty as an officer? I'm not sure how long it will take. Now that my father is retired maybe he and Grandmother can stay with you here for part of the summer. You'll have to work that out with them." He was not surprised that those reserve units that were fully staffed would logically be the first to be pushed into the line of defense.

Lori was old enough to understand the gravity of the situation and thought about it. "Maybe I can stay some with Miss Jean." [A name they all agreed was appropriate for their neighbor]. "She's up for most of the summer."

He did not want to impose his responsibility upon Jean and suggested, "I think it for the best that you stay with your grandparents. Of course, I don't mean for you to not visit with Miss Jean at her convenience."

Things were happening rapidly. He left Maine with the full contingent of his squadron's staff for an airfield staging area in Virginia where they drew added equipment and arms. Ten days later he was in Japan as commander of a squadron of P-51 Mustangs destined for Pusan, South Korea. On his last night in Japan, Ken wrote a letter to Jean:

Somewhere in Japan

July 12, 1950

Dear Jean,

A few words this evening to inform you that our new squadron's move to Korea is imminent. I can't tell you any more than that. Things have been happening so fast I've lost track of time. My permanent APO address is on the envelope of this letter. I can honestly say that I'll be looking forward to your letter(s).

As I look back over the past two years that we've been seeing each other on a regular basis, I want you to know how much I've appreciated the patience and understanding you've given me during that period. Thank you for bringing serenity and harmony into my life. You've done nothing but give to me and asked for nothing in return. I'll try to make it up to you when this thing is over. You have a very generous heart, and I'm fortunate to be the object of your affections.

It may be a while before you hear from me again. The squadron has been refitted with much new equipment so that we can respond to most any type of mission. Please, do not worry about me. We're the best trained and equipped squadron in the theater, and the men are top notch. When we do get to Korea we'll make a difference.

Give my love to Lori the next time you see her. Until next time, all my love.

Ken

He followed with a letter to his parents and one to Lori, trying to project an air of confidence to balance the very serious military situation that then existed in Korea. The North Koreans had blasted their way the full length of the peninsula

172

with the exception of the southern tip around the port city of Pusan where the United Nations forces were hanging on by their toenails. The inept South Korean army was being swept aside with an astonishing display of force by the enemy.

The squadron landed at an airfield west of Pusan with the Mustangs fully armed with fifty-caliber machine gun ammunition, disposable fuel tanks attached and filled, and with two racks of four rockets each fitted to the underside of the wings. They were a potent attack aircraft, and Ken was anxious to have them committed to help turn the tide of battle in their favor. The Pusan Perimeter was in danger of being overrun, and Lieutenant General Walker, Commanding General of the Eighth Army, ordered a defense of the perimeter to the last man. There was no place to retreat to.

Ken's squadron was assigned to the defense of the perimeter and was on call for ground support. They responded instantly with fully loaded Mustangs. Ken interpreted his mission as larger than just ground support, which meant that every plane that went to the line of defense stayed on call until they had used up all of their ordinance against enemy forces. Generally he had his planes flying in grids several miles into enemy territory, taking pains to scrutinize all roads leading to the perimeter. When trucks or tanks were located, they had priority over other targets. They had blasted several tank columns which had to ease some of the pressure against the perimeter.

Every daylight sortie started at the crack of dawn, and Ken always accompanied that sortie looking for targets of opportunity, placing the planes in the vicinity to respond immediately to a call for help from the infantry. Their effort soon earned the respect and admiration of the hard-pressed rifle companies. The pugnacious silver Mustangs circling over the heads of the foot soldiers gave them confidence that they were not alone. Their accuracy in hitting designated targets was exemplary, and reflected Ken's driving force for excellence. When he received excellence he was quick to reward the men's efforts. It was easy for him to say thanks for a job well done. Ken had set the standards for the rest of the squadron to duplicate, so respect and maximum effort came from the top down. Their toll against the enemy proved that his method of command worked well, and morale was high.

The defense of the Pusan Perimeter continued until General MacArthur unleashed a bold strategy against the enemy with an amphibious strike part way up on the Korean peninsula at Inchon. This operation got underway in September. It was designed to act as an anvil against which a heavily armed task force from Pusan driving northward was to be the hammer. If successful, it would cut the enemy forces south of the Inchon-Seoul line from their line of supply.

New orders came for Ken's squadron to protect the flanks of the flying column smashing deep into enemy territory. Spearhead units also used the hard-hitting Mustangs to clear the front of enemy opposition. Throughout daylight hours, one or more of the silver Mustangs was unloading ordnance either at the flanks or at the point of the column speeding toward Seoul. Whenever the planes needed replenishment of ammunitions or fuel, the column commander had a portion of the road cleared so that the planes could use the road as a runway. That technique was responsible for keeping the planes with the column all of the time, increasing their availability.

One day Ken was doing a routine flank patrol when he drew fire from the base of a hill. At first he did not know where it came from until he was hit with several rounds. His wingmate had located the source of the fire and made a sweep against the emplacement with four rockets, which obliterated the stronghold. Ken called his wingman when he came back on formation. "Bulldog One to Bulldog Three, do you read me?"

"Loud and clear, Sir."

"Would you drop down and give me a check? I took several hits, and I'm getting strange engine noises."

"Bulldog One, this is Bulldog Three. You are leaking oil. Try to lower your wheels. I'm not sure if it's hydraulic or engine oil. Perhaps both. Out."

Ken did as he suggested and received a quick response.

"Bulldog One, you have only one landing gear in lock position. That is the port gear. Out"

"Bulldog One to patrol, I'm returning to base at Pusan. Bulldog Three, maintain your patrol and take over command. Out"

"Roger, Bulldog One. Good luck, Sir. Bulldog Three Out."

Since Ken was losing oil, probably from the engine as well as the hydraulic system, he climbed to a higher altitude so that he would have more of a chance to select a crash landing site if he had to ditch.

"Bulldog One to Base."

"Base to Bulldog One, we have you on radar. You're approximately 40 miles from base. Out."

"Thanks, Base. I think I can make it. I have only one landing wheel locked down and am out of hydraulic fluid. I'm going to try for the gravel area beside the tarmac runway so that I won't tear it up. I'll see you guys for lunch. Bulldog One out."

"Good luck, Sir."

While he was making his final approach to bring the wounded Mustang back to base, he thought of the time when Lieutenant Lea Charles had to do the same thing with the same type of aircraft. He repeated her performance by slowing almost to a stall speed, then touched down on one wheel. The wheel collapsed, and he made a perfect belly landing. The ground crew was upon him by the time he moved the cockpit canopy to the rear. They lifted him out of the seat, and he joined his friends for lunch as he had promised.

That afternoon, he returned to his squadron with a rebuilt Mustang and a full complement of ordnance. A new airfield was opened up for the squadron to use as the attacking ground column arrived at Seoul, the Korean capital city. The new field simplified replenishment of ammunition and fuel. The sturdy Mustangs were taking a beating from constant use and sporadic ground fire. Spare parts were slow in reaching them at the front, which kept moving northward. Ken and his pilots thought that they were pushing the safety envelope to a dangerous degree, but they still maintained constant air cover over Seoul.

The forward airbase was shared with a squadron of the new jet, the "Shooting Star" F-80. Ken was impressed with its flowing beauty, and a friend took him up for a spin around the base. The first thing he noted was that it was much quieter in flight than a piston fighter plane, and the response to acceleration was nothing less than phenomenal. It was almost unnerving to experience such speed in such silence. The ride made him a believer.

The slower Mustang was much better suited for flank and ground support missions. The Navy and the Marine Corps were still flying their powerful Corsairs in that role. The two planes were evenly matched for speed but the Mustang was slightly more maneuverable.

The squadron's role as a pathfinder for the attacking column from Pusan disappeared as soon as the column had linked up with allied forces attacking from Inchon. They were ordered to Kimpo Airfield, south of Seoul, to work with the Marines as they began widening their advance around the city. The United Nations forces were ordered to hold in place until further notice. Since there was no active front, Ken requested that his pilots be placed on stand-by and given a few days off for rest. They had been active on the front line constantly for the past two months. Men and equipment both needed an overhaul, and it was granted.

To their surprise, they were given passes to Japan for four days. It was a gift from Heaven. They bummed passage to Japan on empty DC-3s as they made repeated supply runs. The trips back to Japan were frequently made with wounded men who had priority, but at this stage casualties were at a minimum. After a shave and a hot shower in a hotel the Air Force had rented for their use, Ken found a phone and called home. It rang three times, and he was about to hang up when a familiar voice answered: "Hello."

"Lori, Honey, it's so nice to hear your voice again."

"Daddy, where are you?" she cried excitedly. "We've been reading the papers and listening to the radio wondering if you are safe."

"I'm just fine, Honey. I wish I could be there with you. How have things been going for you? You're in my thoughts all the time. Whenever I think of what you may be doing at the cabin it makes me miss you even more. Tell me, have you got enough firewood for the year?"

"Grandmother and Grandpops are staying with me at the cabin while I'm in school. Grandpops told me that they have enough wood in the shed," she reported to him. She sounded so grown up for her age.

"I'm glad. I was worried about that. The fall foliage must be all over by now. I missed that. The fall is my favorite time of year."

"We worry and pray for you every day, Daddy. When are you coming home?"

"Just as soon as we finish the job we started, sweetheart. There's talk that we might be home by Christmas, but that's only a rumor, and you can't rely on them. It's nice to talk with you, Lori. Is Grandmother or Grandpops right there?"

"They left to go shopping, Daddy. They're using the Studebaker coupe. Miss Jean is here with me. She came over to the cabin and offered to stay with me. Do you want to speak to her?" Lori asked him.

"I love you, Lori. Continue to pray for Daddy, for we need all the help we can get. Please let me speak to Miss Jean, Honey."

"I love you too, Daddy."

Jean took the phone and spoke in a wavering voice. "Hello, Ken. Lori and I were just talking about you and here you are on the phone. How nice it is to hear your voice and to know that you're safe."

"I'm glad to have a chance to talk with you, Jean. Almost every day I've received a letter from you and, I can't put into words how important they are. Thank you for being so thoughtful. I'm thankful that you came into my life, and I'm spiritually with you and Lori at the cabin. She sounds like a grown-up girl."

"She's a lovely girl, Ken. You've done a wonderful job with her. She worries more about you than she lets on, but that's only natural. I see so much of you in your daughter. I've seen her a lot since you left for Korea. We go shopping and talk a lot. She's quiet and reserved like her father, and I've come to love her very much. I also love her father."

"It was easy for me to fall in love with you, Jean. You give freely of yourself. I respected you at first, and it grew into something more. Thank you for bringing order and peace to my life. There's a long line of Airmen waiting to use the phone, so I'll hang up now. Tell Lori I love her and wait for me, Jean. I love you."

"I'll be waiting with open arms, my proud pilot. Be careful over there."

The squadron drew winter clothing, for Korean weather can be severe and life-threatening, especially in the mountains where they were heading after the capture of Seoul. The North Korean forces south of Seoul were effectively cut off from their main supply lines, and they were hunted down and destroyed. The United Nations had pushed the North Koreans above the 38th parallel, and General MacArthur was given permission to teach the enemy a lesson, so he ordered an advance to the Yalu River on the Chinese border.

Orders came for Ken's squadron to move their Headquarters to Wonsan on the eastern shore in preparation of the advance to the mountains in the north. The Navy and Marine Corps had also moved their air assets there. The squadron was ordered to remain on an alert status and to assist and to cooperate with the Marines and Army as they advanced into the Chosin Reservoir area.

Chapter Nineteen

Elements of allied infantry forces had crossed the 38th Parallel and worked their way into the Chosin Reservoir by mid-November. Resistance was spotty but severe when it was encountered. Ken's squadron was assigned to support a Regimental Combat Team from the Army's Seventh Infantry Division which was working its way around the eastern side of the frozen Chosin Reservoir. They were the only outfit to reach the Yalu River, and they soon backtracked because they were too small a force to stand alone in enemy territory without supporting arms and a secure supply line.

Severe winter conditions settled over the area with temperatures down to thirty degrees below zero. Just staying alive in such an environment was an achievement. Fighting a fanatical enemy was almost impossible. Special heaters had to be used to keep the oil in planes and trucks from congealing.

Ken and a patrol of four planes from his squadron scouted the area in advance of the Army Regimental Combat Team (RCT) on the eastern side of the Chosin Reservoir. The area was being used as a staging area for two additional battalions of the RCT to join them prior to their movement into the mountainous spine of central Korea. Ken, with his trained eye for vegetation and terrain, was the first to observe something unnatural in the way the vegetation was arranged on a large hill with an excellent view of the surrounding Reservoir area and the Army RCT patrols. He had remembered the hill as having been barren a few days ago and now it was covered with a short coniferous tree that grew in abundance in the valleys and wet areas, but not on top of barren rock.

"Bulldog One to patrol. I'm going down to inspect that prominent elevation at close range. There's something out of place there. Maintain a circular formation with a five mile radius, out."

"Bulldog Two to Bulldog One, Roger and out."

Ken dropped his speed and came at the hillside, almost touching the vegetation with his propeller. He saw tracks in the snow, and in one spot saw movement beneath the snow cover. A second run with the sun at his back revealed several places where he was able to distinguish either machine gun or mortar barrels with light cover of snow over them. His gut reaction was that the hill was being used as an artillery observation point. He made a sharp turn away from the hill and dropped his sights on a concentration of the small evergreens and fired two rockets into the mass.

A large puff of snow covered the hillside. Debris and metallic parts settled on top of the ground along with several men who desperately tried to hide in the snow from the Mustang. His fears were validated; the vegetation hid enemy formations and strongholds. He made another sweep of the hillside and fired two more rockets and at the same time sprayed the area with his six fifty-caliber machine guns. He saw more human figures uncovered by the attack and climbed steeply out of range of any potential anti-air weapon they might possess.

The most important thing now to do was to call and let intelligence know what he had uncovered. "Bulldog One to Command Control. Repeat, Bulldog One to Command Control. Do you read me? Out."

"Command Control to Bulldog One, we copy."

"Bulldog One to Command Control. I have uncovered a massive and cleverly camouflaged concentration of enemy forces located on Hill Number 611 of the Seventh Division Area Map with coordinates H-14. Enemy has maintained excellent fire discipline. I have not experienced any return fire. They appear to be more interested in making themselves invisible than taking me out, which they could have done. Bulldog One out."

"Bulldog One to Ground Control, did you monitor my transmission to Command Control?"

"Ground Control to Bulldog One, roger. We heard and understand. Do you have enough fuel to make a wider sweep of the surrounding area? Ground Control out."

"Bulldog One to Ground Control. Affirmative and Out."

Breaking his four planes into two two-plane teams to work in a semi-circle of up to fifty miles radius adjacent to the proposed line of advance of the Army's RCT, Ken and his partner took the northern portion of the circle, flying in a loose formation. They were unable to identify anything they could confirm except for tracks in the snow, which were numerous, and at this late hour of the day with the sun ready to set, cast long shadows. All four pilots reported seeing the same thing. They all duly reported to Ground Control and to Command Control back at Wonsan. Something was up, and the infantry was walking into a known enemy of undetermined strength.

That night, Ken crawled into his sleeping bag exhausted and worried. He could not dispel a lingering premonition that something was wrong. He had discussed it with his ground crews and ordered every plane to be checked and double-checked for serviceability and to be fueled and armed ready for takeoff at dawn. He wanted to give the very best possible cover and support to the soldiers on the ground. He had a feeling that hell was about to let loose. Some of the Navy and Marine squadrons thought that he was carrying a "hunch" too far, but on the morning of November 28, 1950, his precautions were vindicated.

Early that morning, several divisions of the Chinese People's Army hit and destroyed every isolated small unit of UN forces in the Chosin Mountain region and in the western portions of the peninsula. The Marine and Army units in the Chosin Reservoir area had only one road for supply or for withdrawal, and they began to concentrate their forces by giving ground slowly.

The under strength Army RCT on the eastern side of the Reservoir was hard pressed and had to pull back from its extended position and refrained from placing outposts too far from Central Control. They were ill-prepared to defend themselves against a determined large force. The silver Mustangs of Ken's squadron were powerful reminders to the men on the ground that they were not alone. The strategy of the Chinese was to annihilate the UN forces by cutting the main supply road into small strips so that a small, yet numerically superior force could command control of the lifeline of the UN forces.

It just so happened that the Chinese accidentally ran into the Army RCT which blocked their attempt to sever the supply road south of the Chosin Reservoir, perhaps the most vital portion of their strategy. Ken's Mustangs worked valiantly to stop the wave upon wave of Chinese soldiers. The RCT was in danger of being completely isolated. The planes could not cover every perimeter at the same time.

Ken had recognized that potential and sent a steady relay of fully armed Mustangs to their support. The carnage was horrific, and the hordes continued to storm out of the northeast. He maintained an overhead flight from dawn to sunset. For four days and nights the valiant Army RCT absorbed punishing losses and dealt the enemy better than they received. On that last day, wounded had been collected and placed in trucks ready for a last-ditch breakout from their positions to the main supply road. The road was held by an unknown number of enemy, but it was the only route of withdrawal open to them with all of the wounded they had to take care of.

"Bulldog One to Ground Control. Your small column of trucks is completely surrounded by large numbers of enemy soldiers. The route south has one small bridge near an inlet from the reservoir. We will do our best to cover your flanks to that point and will blast a hole in their defense, blocking the road ahead of you. Good luck, soldiers. Out"

"Ground Control to Bulldog One. This will be our final transmission as the radio truck engine has quit. Thank God for those beautiful Mustangs overhead. Please contact Headquarters that we're coming out. We are out of ammunition, medical supplies and food; we haven't eaten in two days. Tell them we're doing the best we can. Again, a heartfelt thanks from this command for a job well done. Ground Control out."

"Bulldog One, to Ground Control. Roger and out."

Ken felt sick. The courage and guts of the infantrymen below deserved better than they were getting. He called for his wingman to follow him down for a sweep of the flanks of the slow moving column of trucks. He was taking heavy ground fire as he laid a swath of machine gun fire close to the trucks carrying the wounded. Several shells pierced the sheet metal of his cockpit, rocking the plane sideways and hitting him on the left side of his body, slamming him against the canopy, disorienting him. He was unable to lift his left arm and controlled the plane with the foot pedals and stick in his right fist. He instinctively pulled the stick to climb away from the ground fire.

"Bulldog One to Bulldog Two. I've been hit, but will stay with you. Call in another flight to cover for us. Those men on the ground have got only one chance of making it, and we've got to give them that chance, regardless of cost. Out."

The wingman called in for relief and described the situation as "desperate in the extreme." The two pilots had finished making another sweep of the flanks, and at the point position they saw hand grenades being exploded in the truck bodies filled with wounded men. They could not imagine the grotesque slaughter taking place. Ken let go with his remaining rockets at the front of the column and swung back over to use up his remaining machine gun ammunition.

"Bulldog One to Bulldog Two. I'm out of ammunition and will drop fuel tanks on enemy concentrations down the road. Out."

"Bulldog Two to Bulldog One. Roger Sir. I'll stay on station until another patrol relieves me and will try to catch up with you. Your plane is damaged. If you have to ditch, be sure to turn on your transponder and I'll find you. Out."

Ken was feeling weak and nauseous, afraid he would vomit in the cockpit. Angry at his limitations when he needed them the most, he made one more pass over the burning column of trucks. He had to see how badly the situation was for himself. Small clusters of American soldiers, some dragging wounded men on the hoods of dismantled trucks and jeeps, were trying to cross the frozen ice to escape the horror at the inlet. The image of wounded soldiers dying in a pyre of fire and the added desecration of being blown to bits from countless hand grenades thrown by the Chinese hordes fueled his rage. He could not hear the cries of pain, but he could imagine it. Twice he buzzed the enemy even though his ammunition was expended, but at least, it momentarily averted their attention from the wounded men.

The scene below so enraged him that he no longer felt his wounds even though he could not move his left arm. Blood began to collect on the floor underneath his feet. He then turned and flew south toward Wonsan. Looking back several times, he was able to lock the scene into his consciousness. A complete sense of helplessness angered him that he could not have prevented the tragedy. For an hour Ken had fought drowsiness and occasional lapses of awareness on his way back to the airfield. His last conscious thought was bringing the crippled aircraft onto the runway and touching down to Mother Earth.

"Bulldog to Ground Control, I'm on approach and will need medical assistance and emergency crew."

"Ground Control to Bulldog One, we copy you Colonel and are ready to assist you. Out."

"Bulldog to Ground Control, I'm losing altitude and am low on fuel... not sure if I can stay alert..."

"Ground Control to Bulldog One. Roger, we have you on radar. Keep your nose up slightly. Do you copy?"

"Ground Control to Bulldog One. Do you copy?"

"Ground Control to Bulldog One. Do you copy?"

"Ground Control to Bulldog One. Do you copy?"

Chapter Twenty

May, 1965

The sun was casting long shadows across the airfield. Gone were the days when the earth trembled from the launching of heavily loaded bombers thundering down the runway filled with anxious young airmen holding their breaths and silently praying that the aircraft would take flight before crashing into the forest that surrounded the field. Now the planes were gone, and any remaining vestige that they ever existed remained in piles of rusted metal slowly deteriorating and returning back to Mother Earth from whence they came. The B-17s and B-24s were gone. The concrete runways were slowly being reclaimed by farmers growing crops. A few of the Quonset huts which housed the airmen were now rusted relics with their roofs fallen in. They had been placed in close proximity around the square operational control tower and observation platform that was the heart and soul of the activity.

Nothing remained as it had once been, but in the hearts of those who had lived the dream, the memories and images from the past were still vivid and alive. When they answer life's last muster call, the world will lose that direct link to a time when the world was on fire, and nations were intent on destroying each other. Those who survived the melting pot were a generation of men and women the likes of which the world may never see again.

From the depths of a prolonged and cruel depression, they volunteered to fight for their country and were proud to wear the uniform. They came from the cities, the farms, and

185

from the lonely isolated hills and valleys across the land to merge together into the most powerful instrument of justice ever assembled to destroy evil where it threatened free nations. Citizen soldiers temporarily took up the cause of liberty and defeated two of the most militaristic nations in the world, Japan and Germany, on the field of battle.

Afterwards, they shed their uniforms and began the task of rebuilding the nation and raising their families. They suffered the horrors of the war in lonely silence because their families could never comprehend just how it had been, and the veterans collectively refused to discuss it. Their silence was a tribute to the valor and unquenchable courage that had sustained them. Strong men and women answered the challenge. They had been victorious, but, alas, the cost was high. Those who witnessed the clash of giants would never forget how it had been.

Colonel Kenneth Morgan was a charter member of the brotherhood of warriors who had suffered and survived the ravages of war. He was drawn to this place once again to reminisce. Ken now stood on the observation platform of the severely weathered control tower, leaning against the railing to support himself. He slowly cleaned his pipe and filled it with Half and Half tobacco. He had returned to the airfield for one last glimpse of the place where he sprang from a young man to a mature adult. The Zippo lighter he had carried all through the wars still worked, and he held it to the well-tamped tobacco. His presence at this place, and at this time, was to attend the twentieth anniversary of the end of the war. It was a fitting time for those who shared its many secrets and had suppressed the memories, to remember with those brethren who had also served. Tears of painful memories and that old angst of feeling alone and insignificant that had been such a common part of the generation he represented, still lingered.

The reunion gave the veterans with graying and thinning hair a chance to embrace their never forgotten brothers, and it also gave them the opportunity to share the times with their loved ones so that maybe, just maybe, they could better understand how it had been. On many occasions, when reflections and echoes from the past were overwhelming, it was difficult for the veteran to hide his sad eyes and the uncontrollable tremor of lips. And once again they were *little boys afraid of the dark.*

The reunion also gave the veterans a chance to say goodbye, perhaps for the last time, to those who were buried in a foreign land, forgotten and forsaken by the world, except for the select few who witnessed their sacrifice. Ken Morgan had tried to live a life worthy of the sacrifice of Joey Salmon, Jim Reams, Lew Whalen, Harry Drew, and countless others whose memory they had returned to England to honor. The fallen remained forever young, and that is how they were remembered by their comrades. Memories evoked much pain and sorrow, and perhaps that was the way it should be – lest we forget, lest we forget! Their courage and valor knew no equal.

* * *

Ken broke free of his quiet reverie back to yesterday when a soft voice called to him from the foot of the stairs below. He turned to see his wife of twelve years, Jean; their twelve-year-old son, Kenneth, Jr.; and his lovely daughter Ensign Lori Morgan of the United States Coast Guard.

"It was getting late and we were worried about you," Jean said, taking him into her arms as he stepped off the platform. She could read his thoughts and saw the sadness in his eyes disappear as his family quietly surrounded him. Jean had seen that same stare several times over the years, and she had tried to dispel the ugly images with all the love she held for him. Their marriage in 1953 had been a whole new beginning of a relationship that continued to grow for both of them. She had walked into his life one cold fall evening in need of a helping hand. She had found that and more in the strong and studious Kenneth Morgan, and worked tirelessly to create an atmosphere where her beloved husband could be released from the ugly memories that had held him captive for so long.

Twelve-year-old Ken, Jr., had inherited his father's gentle demeanor and went to his father's side. "Are you all right, Father?" he had asked, feeling uncomfortable seeing his father so sad.

Ken pulled him and Lori into the embrace with his right arm and with the artificial limb that replaced his left arm lost in the Korean War. "I'm okay, Son. Don't be alarmed if you see emotions on this trip that you've never seen before. One of the reasons I was so anxious to make this reunion was to share with all of you where I went to war as a very young man and survived a much older and matured human being. This is the field where I flew Flying Fortresses with the Eighth Air Force. There's little of note to show you, but this control tower was the center of our existence. I can almost hear the drone of heavy bombers lifting off and landing after a long trip over Germany to bomb a strategic target. Some planes that made it back were filled with wounded and dead airmen..."

Jean lifted her head and kissed him on both of his eyes. "We are so proud of you and the men who served with you. I knew that this reunion would be an emotional mountain for you to climb. I'm not wise enough to hope that you can just forget all that has taken place, but I pray that our love for you is strong enough to overshadow those dark recesses of your mind."

"Mother has said it well, Daddy," Lori softly replied, still clinging to the family embrace. "Your sacrifice and courage have been acknowledged by the Medal Of Honor you wear around your neck. How proud we were of you when President Truman placed it there in the Oval Office."

"I'm a lucky man, and I'm so proud of my family," he replied in a low voice. "I'm ready to return to the inn with you so that we can get ready for the evening's activities. I can leave this place now. In a way, I never left it. I've carried it in my heart for twenty years."

That evening several hundred men, women, and children from the squadron Ken had commanded during the war gathered at a country inn in Anglia County to renew old acquaintances and to introduce their loved ones to their comrades.

Ken had showered and shaved and changed into a clean blue serge suit Jean had selected for him. She placed the MOH sash around his neck and kissed him. He was still a handsome man. Lori had put on her dress white uniform - a newly graduated Ensign from the Coast Guard Academy. She undid young Ken's neck tie and redid it for him.

"This is a night to look your best, Junior, so suffer in silence," she smiled at him. "If you act as good as you look, you'll do just fine."

He returned her smile. "You look swell in that white uniform, Lori. Some of my friends have a crush on you." He grasped his sister's outstretched hand and walked beside her behind their parents who made an attractive couple.

The banquet room was filling up when Ken and his family arrived. They were ushered to a table near the small stage at the front of the room. There was much friendly bantering and hand-waving. It settled down as the quests were served their meals of fish, chicken, or steak. A half hour later, a short portly man walked up to the microphone on the stage and held his hands up for silence.

"Friends and veterans of the Tenth Squadron of the 200th Bomber Group. I'm Mayor John Hadley, and it is my pleasure to welcome you proud veterans and families to our community. How fortunate we were to have been the hosts for our gallant American Airmen. They quickly became our boys as much as they are yours. We took you to our hearts, and you have never left us. The sound of the bombers coming and going were like music to our ears.

"We shared your sorrow when fewer planes returned to base than left that same morning. How can we pay back that noble sacrifice? The answer is 'we cannot.' There is a granite monument in the Marne region of northern France at a cemetery for World War I American soldiers. The monument pays tribute to the young Americans: *Virtue and Courage are Their Own Monument and Reward*. I believe that sentiment is also appropriate for another generation of young Americans who made the supreme sacrifice for their English brethren.

"I hope that we have been worthy. I know that many of us who cherish the memories of young, cocky Yanks who died in the prime of life, have never left us. Many of us believe that their souls are still out there at the field.

"I now have the distinct privilege and unique honor to introduce to you a man whom we, without exception, are proud to call one of our very own. He wears the Medal of Honor for gallantry above and beyond the call of duty in Korea, 1950. Please give a welcome to Colonel Kenneth Morgan."

Ken slowly rose from the table and walked up to the microphone, where he adjusted it a little higher. He stood silent for several seconds looking from side to side, acknowledging the rousing applause and whistles that greeted him. He was not ashamed of the artificial arm with a set of stainless steel tongs that replaced his left hand, but he became self-conscious when he had to explain it over and over again. He held out both of his arms to acknowledge the audience.

"Friends, families of friends, and guests. I'm not much at making speeches, but on this solemn occasion, I wanted to tell you how proud I was to have served with all of you, and to let those families of loved ones lost to the world, just how much their memory remains within our hearts. We mourn their passing, and we must never forget what they stood for – their legacy of courage and commitment should always guide our footsteps. I ask, in their name, for a few moments of silence to remember our fallen heroes whom we still love and cherish..."

The audience bent their heads as one in silent prayer, remembering those young men whom some in the audience never knew.

"I'm sure those young souls are sharing in our remembrances at this reunion." He paused a moment and made eye contact with Jean. "On a lighter note, I want to introduce my very special family to you. My lovely wife, Jean, our son, Kenneth, Jr., and our daughter, Lori. This attractive lady wearing the uniform of an Ensign in the Coast Guard was my inspiration for 'Sweet Lori', a name carried by three different Flying Fortresses." Lori acknowledged the applause of the crowd and blushed, winking at her father.

"Now, I want to turn the rest of the evening over to some special ladies that you veterans will remember with great affection. Ladies and gentlemen, I proudly give you Lieutenant Lea Charles Colson and her associates, Lieutenant Martha Gibson and Captain Terry White, otherwise known as the THREE WAFS." Ken held out his left arm to Lea and her associates as they climbed up to the stage. Lea kissed Ken on the cheek before he stepped off the stage, and then turned to the audience.

"We thought it would be fun to play and sing some of the songs that were popular during the war. Before we begin though, I want you to meet a very special man in my life, my husband, a veteran sailor, Matt Colson. Another man in my life is a recent graduate of the United States Military Academy, my son, Second Lieutenant Donald Charles." She pointed to a table near the edge of the stage. Matt Colson was a short, stocky man with dark hair as contrasted to Lieutenant Charles, tall and slim and straight as an arrow.

"The staff at the inn has told us that they will roll back the room divider so that you'll have a chance to dance to the tunes of long ago. How could we ever forget them? I hope you enjoy our selections. Thank you." Lea took her place at the grand piano on the stage and arranged the microphone. Her associates took seats beside her with their violins.

They began a litany of familiar tunes including:

NOW IS THE HOUR, FARAWAY PLACES, WE'LL MEET AGAIN..., SOMEWHERE ALONG THE WAY, WHEN I GROW TOO OLD TO DREAM, and others.

The dance floor began to fill. Lieutenant Charles stopped at Ken's table, "It's nice to see all of you again. Your Medal Of Honor will always have my respect, Colonel."

"Thank you, Lieutenant," Ken answered. "I'm glad that you could fit this occasion into your busy schedule. I know your mother is very proud to show you off."

"And I expect that you, too, have been proud to do the same with Sweet Lori," he smiled at Lori. "May I have the honor of this dance, Ensign Morgan?"

Lori returned his smile and offered her arm to be escorted to the floor.

"Well, Junior," Ken said, standing up. "You can hold the fort while I show off your lovely mother to the envy of every man in the hall."

Jean blushed, as was her way of accepting her husband's compliment. "I'll be honored, Colonel." She took his left hand and fell into his arms, placing her head against his chest, once they reached the floor. "Lori and Donald make an attractive couple. What do you think? Are they serious with each other?"

Ken kissed her on the top of her head. "I'm going to bet that within a year they'll be engaged."

Music and merriment filled the small English inn. It was an important time for the veterans to share with their loved ones a little bit of what it had been like. The spirits of those who died were silent witnesses to the solemn occasion. The veterans with their gray hair and wider waist belts stood in stark contrast to the spirits of their dead comrades who were forever young men in their late teens and early twenties. They heard the laughter and they understood the tribute given in their names, but they watched with sad eyes and wished for what might have been...

THE END

Other Historical Romance Novels
BY
Clifton LaBree

A Song for Lisa   A Historical Romance

This is the story of a young American woman captured by the Japanese in the Philippines, 1941. Like most prisoners, she was brutalized and sadistically treated with a cruel disregard for human life. Three years later, Lisa and her companions had reached the low point of starvation and abuse .....

Lake of Three Sorrows   A Historical Romance

A warm spiritually uplifting story of courage, commitment, and sacrifice. This is the story of Dale Cooper, a battle-weary American soldier who served in two world wars.

Flickering Flame (Colonial Series Book One)

A historical novel, about the Cullen family who settled in Portsmouth, New Hampshire, and their participation in events prior to the French and Indian War. Freedom and opportunity were on the march, but it extracted a heavy price. Frontier settlers were ruthlessly killed and butchered by rampaging Indians lead by French officers and Jesuit priests who frequently incited them to greater levels of inhumanity...

Raising the Torch (Colonial Series Book Two)

A continuation of the saga from Flickering Flame, Colonial Series book one, of the Cullen family in Colonial Portsmouth. This is a moving story of love and sacrifice when a small colony had the audacity to fight for independence from their motherland...

Non-Fiction Books

By

Clifton LaBree

New Hampshire's General John Stark, Live Free or Die: Death Is Not the Greatest of Evils

Publisher - Fading Shadows Imprint

A fresh look at one of America's staunchest defenders of liberty and freedom. John Stark was a courageous New Hampshire citizen-soldier who fought in both, the French and Indian War, and the Revolutionary War. His pursuit of leadership excellence on the battlefield distinguished him as one of the most successful combat commanders of the war, and one of the least appreciated.

His selflessness, modest life style, and devotion to the cause of freedom are an inspiration that time has not diminished. He remains today the embodiment of the frugal, independent, and cantankerous New Hampshire Yankee.

Gentle Warrior, General Oliver Prince Smith, USMC

Published by - Kent State University Press. Kent, Ohio, 2001

The Story of one of the United States Marine Corps best General Officer. His flawless performance in Korea is a story that needed to be told.

FADING SHADOWS IMPRINT

Fading Shadows Imprint was established to bring to the public books of historical events and portraits of people enduring tragic circumstances of by-gone days. Hopefully, they will generate a deep appreciation and respect for the exceptionalness of the United States of America, and an appreciation for the sacrifice and selflessness of those who valiantly served for liberty and freedom.

The characters are fictional, but the historical events and dates have been seriously researched and are factually presented. Some books feature incidents during the French and Indian Wars as well as the War for Independence.

World Wars I and II are eras rich in stories that beg to be told. I've tried to pay tribute to the collective courage and heroism, often unheralded, that has defined Americans in every engagement. It was a time when the immortality of dreams and aspirations were defended by the blood of young men and women. There is a beautiful monument and cemetery in a small French village where thousands of white crosses and Stars-of-David are set in perfect alignment, honoring thousands of American soldiers who gave their last full measure. A large granite slab bearing mute witness to their sacrifice has the following words chiseled in stone: TIME WILL NOT DIM THE GLORY OF THEIR DEEDS. Another monument reads: VIRTUE AND COURAGE ARE THEIR OWN MONUMENT AND REWARD. Those simple words define the American soldier from the dark days of the Revolutionary War to the present. They are an American treasure, unique in the history of the world.

Every generation has its own signature and characteristics that uniquely define them. The World War II generation is defined by the immortality of the ideals and truth they gallantly defended.

The United States has freely given precious blood and treasure to defend the rights of man to be free, and we have never asked for anything in return. No other nation on the planet has sacrificed so much for the noble virtues of liberty and freedom. We hope that the selections offered by Fading Shadows Imprint will touch your hearts and generate a deeper appreciation and love for our country.

www.ingramcontent.com/pod-product-compliance
Lightning Source LLC
Chambersburg PA
CBHW071311200626
46813CB00015B/1519